A MALICE
Love

A NOVEL BY
BIANCA

CHAPTER 1

Kambridge 'Kam' Lewis

*B*eep!

I rolled my eyes at the sound of the door chime going off, letting me know that someone had walked into the store. I had just bit into my sandwich that I got from the sub shop that was two doors down. I had been working all day, and hadn't had anything to eat.

"WHAT I GOT TO DO TO GET SOME MOTHAFUCKIN' SERVICE IN THIS BITCH," a deep ass voice boomed throughout the store.

"Nun-uh. I know this ghetto ass nigga didn't," I whispered to myself as I looked at the camera.

This nigga got to be from that other side of Chicago. The side that my daddy had forbade me from going to.

"AYE!" he yelled, and started beating on the counter.

I took a deep breath as I walked slowly from the back. I wondered who got shot and killed now. That seemed like the only thing that I printed these days, 'Rest in Peace' shirts.

"You really have to be out of your mind coming in my establishment with all that ghetto mess. You can take that shit back on the other side of Chicago where you came from," I snapped.

"Had you not been back there suckin' dick, your ass could have been out here doing what the fuck you supposed to do, and I wouldn't have had to be out here damn near servicing myself," he snapped right back.

"Excuse me!"

"You're excused to go wipe that cum from around your lips. Stop suckin' dick during work hours, and you would be able to make some fucking money around this joint," he said, looking around.

I turned around and looked in the mirror and saw that I had mayo around my lips, and I was instantly embarrassed. I wiped my mouth and turned back towards him.

"For future references, before you start going off, you need to read. It's a big ass sign directly in front of you that says, and I quote, RING BELL IF NO ONE IS AT THE COUNTER. Now what you want?" I rolled my eyes as I slammed my notepad on the counter.

Ding! He tapped the bell, and I sighed so hard and rolled my eyes again. This nigga was getting on my last nerve.

"You tryin' way too hard, prep school. You look like you went to a prep school. Yo' ass probably ain't never been to the slums."

"What that got to do with placing an order? Please place an order so I can finish⊠"

"Finish suckin' dick. Aight. Look. I want about fifty t-shirts."

"I wasn't sucking dick, but whatever."

He stared at me like I had shit on my face, and I stared back at him like he had shit on his.

"Don't interrupt me while I'm talking, shorty. Write this down. I don't want you to fuck nothing up, and I have to come back here and rough yo' lil' preppy ass up."

"What does it look like I'm doing, sir? Stop calling me preppy! I'm not!"

He chuckled. "Aight, look. I want the shirts to say Rich Cutz, and spell that Cutz with a z, prep school. Here goes the design right here. Put Rich on one side of it, and Cutz on the other. You got that?"

"Sure. Anything else?"

"Nah. I want these shirts by tomorrow too," he ordered.

"Want or need because--"

"Let me change that. I *need* these shirts tomorrow, shorty. You ain't doing shit else anyway. You can get this shit done by tomorrow."

"First of all, sir! MY store may not look like much to you, but I have more than just you waiting on shirts. You can't come in here requesting... Look, I can tell you right now, this is not going to be done by--"

"Well, you need to hire some help if you can't do rush orders."

I closed my eyes and counted to ten in my head before I responded to his arrogant ass.

"I'll do it, but it's going to be extra. What's your name, and what color t-shirts you want? Do you know what style you want? Do you want glitter, or anything else on your letters?"

"Do I look like I want some damn glitter on my fucking letters, preppy? I'on know what type of shirts I want. I ain't know they had different types of shirts, and money ain't no issue. The color going to be black, and put the letters and design in white. Malice is my name."

Malice is the perfect name for this arrogant and rude ass nigga, I thought to myself as I stared at him.

"Yep, you are thinking right. My attitude matches my fucking name. Now, explain to me what type of shirts you talkin' bout."

I turned around and pulled out the example shirts. I spread them out on the counter.

"This is a polo style shirt, women's, jersey, and a regular t-shirt. The jerseys and polo style shirts are a little more than the regular t-shirts. Since I'm sure you are going to be selling these, you might want to get these regular t-shirts because the sizes fit better. The regular style shirts are ten dollars per shirt."

"Um, what about these jerseys? How much are they? These button-up jerseys are fly as shit."

"The button-up jerseys are eighteen dollars per jersey, and the regular jerseys are fifteen."

"Aight, I'll take the button up jerseys. Eighteen bucks for fifty jerseys should be about nine hundred dollars, and I'll just bump it up to fifteen hundred dollars for your troubles, Ms....?"

"Kam... my name is Kam," I whispered.

My mind was completely blown on how fast he calculated that

shit in his head. When he did that shit, it made me look at him different. I looked him up and down, and it looked like he was the same height as my brother, which was about six feet even. He had on a t-shirt, which showed off his muscular build. He wasn't light skinned, and he wasn't dark. He was somewhere in the middle. He had a beard, a small curly fro, a tiny mustache, and that shit was lined to perfection. His eyes were kind of closed, and I ain't know if he had been smoking or what, but now that I was looking past his arrogant and rude ass behavior, he was sexy as hell.

"Prep School, stop staring at me like that, and take this damn money out my hand before my damn hand fall off. You tripping," Malice snapped.

I didn't realize that he had pulled out a wad of twenty-dollar bills, and was dangling them in my face. I cleared my throat and grabbed the bills and counted them. It took me a minute to count out the seventy-five twenties he gave me, but I was definitely excited about the extra money. My business was doing good, but any extra money I got, I was appreciative.

"Sorry, I'll have them ready for you tomorrow at--"

"You going to have them ready by tomorrow morning. See you tomorrow, Prep School."

Before I could even protest, he had turned and walked out of the damn store. I could see that he had a gun in the small of his back which let me know that this nigga was a fucking thug. The twenties, adding the money up quickly, and the gun screamed drug dealer.

I went into the back to start on his shirts. It was only going to take me a few hours because I had a huge machine where I could press at least five shirts at a time. I knew I could get it done, but I just had orders in front of Malice's ugly ass. I loved my business, but the work was very tedious at times. He bothered my nerves, but what bothered me the most was when he kept calling me 'Prep School.' I was definitely trying not to give off that vibe because... long story short, I hated my life sometimes. You can thank my dad for that.

My name is Kambridge Lewis, but my family calls me Kam. I'm close with my siblings. I have an older brother, Kade, and younger sister, Kalena. We are the children of Judge Kason Lewis, who so proudly locks up the drug dealers in the mean streets, and our mother is Tracey Lewis, and she is the vice president of human resources for a big ass company. As long as I could remember, my parents had me in private schools. I was seriously one of the few black girls in my school, and you would think that they would want to be cool, but that was not the case at all. They were real life mean girls, and that was not me. Well, living in Chicago, you gotta be mean because some of these niggas are straight up disrespectful, like Malice, but there were some that were worse than him. The only time I ever encounter them is when they waltz they ass in my store being very demanding.

The reason I said that I hated my life sometimes is because my dad seriously made it unbearable. I'm twenty-two years old, and I still live in the house with him. He won't let me live on my own. He insists that our house is big enough for me to continue to live there. He has me on a curfew like I am a child. That's why I try not to take orders too late because he will blow a gasket if I stay out late. Like I said before, even if I wanted to go on the other side of Chicago, I was forbidden to. I took an order over there one time, and my dad nearly had a heart attack, chewed me out, and had my mom not been there, he probably would have done something else. Luckily, she was there.

Beep!

I looked at the camera and smiled as my boyfriend of ten years came in the door. It sounds funny that at age twenty-two, I've been with someone for ten years, but it's true. I've been going to school with Connor since we were in grade school. At age twelve, we sealed our relationship with a kiss after his first basketball game. Connor was smart just like me, and I loved him so much. He treated me with so much respect. He was so loyal, and despite his parents' hatred towards me, he didn't let that stop him from being with me. Connor was white, and his parents didn't like me. Well, they didn't like black people, and especially the fact that both of my parents' salary brought in half a million a year, which doubled what his parents made. His mom was a 'homemaker' as she called it, and his dad was an optometrist. There were a couple of things that I absolutely didn't like, and one of them was his racist ass friends. They drove me crazy, and I couldn't stand to be around them.

My brother hated Connor, and he always said that 'birds of a feather, flock together.' He told me that if that 'white nigga' hangs around racist mothafuckas, then he was racist too, and there was nothing that I could say to change his mind. Honestly, Connor has never said anything racist around me; even when he has been angry as hell at me, nothing of the sort came out of his mouth. Also, he would tell me to keep my scars covered, which was one of my biggest insecurities. That is one of the reasons why I wore a lot of makeup and never wore my arms or back out.

"Hey! My chocolate beauty! How has your day been?" Connor asked, stepping into the back loosening the knot in his tie.

Connor was the most handsome white boy ever. Some people would say he looks mixed, but he's fully white. I think it's the black hair that gives off that mixed vibe. Connor is six feet two, thick, and toned. Just like I like them. He could have easily played football in college, but that wasn't his thing. He was a 'pretty white boy.' You know. The white boys that acted like they were too good to do anything, and thought he was God's gift to women. He was also the reason why none of the white girls liked me. They thought that I was 'beneath' him, like we all weren't in the same damn school that cost our parents fifty thousand a year.

"My day was⊠" I started.

"I know your day was easy, so let me tell you about my day. I got three cases sitting on my desk that I just want to throw away," he said, cutting me off.

That was one other thing that always made me mad with him. He would ask me questions, and then make the shit about him. He did that shit all through high school and college. We went to the same college. He got his degree in Pre-law and Criminal Justice, with a minor in English, while I got my degree in Business with a minor in Music. He always thought that his degree was more important than mine, to the point where he would just assume my classes were easy and shit. He was a Paralegal, so he always had interesting stories for when he got off from work. He is currently studying to take the bar exam to get into law school. I will be glad when he takes that shit, so I can stop hearing about it.

"Did you hear me? It's like you zoned out," he said.

"Yeah, I heard you," I replied, lying.

"What's Rich Cutz? Whose order is this," he said, looking at the neatly folded jerseys.

"Guy came in here earlier and paid me extra to have these jerseys done in the morning. I only have a few more to do."

"What guy? Did you know him? How much extra?" He fired off question after question.

Connor is so jealous. Sometimes it's cute, and sometimes it's truly annoying. He swears that some black man is going to come and sweep me off my feet, and leave him in the cold. I have to constantly reassure him that I don't want anybody but him.

"His name is Malice, and no, I didn't know him. He gave me fifteen hundred dollars because it's a rush order."

"FIFTEEN HUNDRED DOLLARS! Was he black? Did you give him some pussy or ass?"

"First, stop yelling in here! Second, why would I give him some pussy, when I'm not even giving you any pussy? Third, are you insinuating that I'm a prostitute because…wait a minute, those two questions together just don't even make sense. You need to leave your stress at work, and stop taking it out on me," I snapped on him. "Yes, he was black!"

"I'm sorry, Kammy! You know how I get sometimes. I don't want to lose you," he said, walking over and kissing me on my forehead, and then kissing me on my lips.

"Connor, you're not going to lose me. Please stop being jealous."

"You're right. I'm sorry. I'm going down to Hunter's to study for the bar exam. You want to come?"

Hunter was one of his racist ass friends who lived in the basement of his parents' home. He had a big ass room in his house, where they often had parties, but mostly used it for a study room. At least that's what Connor said. I had enough of Hunter in high school and college to the point where if I never saw him again, it would be too soon. So, I've never been to his home, ever. They may try to hold me hostage or something.

"Seriously." I rolled my eyes at him. "I honestly don't know why you keep asking me that question when you know I'm not stepping foot in that racist fool's house. I haven't before, and I don't plan to start."

"Hunter is not racist, Kam." He defended his friend like he always does.

"Con, if you don't think those *jokes* that Hunter tell isn't racist, then☒"

"Then what?" He glared at me.

I rolled my eyes as I placed Malice's last jersey in the box.

"Look, Kam, I don't want to fight. I'm sorry. I'll only be over there for a few hours. I'll swing by your house on the way home. Is that cool?"

"Is Holly going to be there?" I asked.

I hated asking about her, but I knew that she secretly loved

Connor. She was a paralegal too. It's bad enough that they worked together, but they also study together for the bar exam.

"I don't know, but don't start that mess, Kambridge. You know I only got eyes for you, and I am so in love with you. I'm going to get out of here. The quicker I can get out of here, the quicker that I can come over and cuddle up with you," he smiled.

He placed a kiss on my lips, and it instantly started getting deeper. The shit felt so good that I wanted to bend over and let him fuck me right then. Connor's lips were small and pink, but he still was a good kisser.

"Can I get some ass tonight?" he whispered like we weren't the only people in the room.

"Of course, baby! You know it!" I replied.

He smacked me on my ass before he left. I hollered out for him to lock the door on his way out. I wasn't taking any more orders this evening. As I was cleaning up the back room, I thought about Connor's dick being in my ass. I wondered could I still call myself a virgin since I still had my cherry. I told Connor that I wanted to give my virginity to my husband, but we could have anal sex. I know that it's weird as shit, but it's something so he won't go out and fuck bitches like Holly's slut ass. We give each other head, and I let him fuck me in my ass. That should be good enough until we get married.

After I finished cleaning the back room, I walked around my store to make sure everything was good. I set the alarm, locked the store, and headed to my white Audi RS7. This was a graduation gift from my parents when I graduated from college. I cranked the car and stared at my store, Kam's Tees. I seriously opened this store a month after I graduated from college. This is seriously my pride and joy. I used my own money to open this store. I mean, it's not like my dad wouldn't help, but I wanted to show him that I was responsible. Responsible enough to have my own damn house, and do other things that normal twenty-two-year-olds do. The time on my dash told me that it was eight, so I still had time to catch a movie before my 11:30 stupid ass curfew. On the weekends, I had to be in the house at twelve, a whopping thirty minutes difference from the weekdays. *No daughter of Judge Lewis will be out in the streets like she is a streetwalker.* I heard my dad's voice in my head every time I wanted to skip curfew, and just deal with whatever consequence. I sighed heavily before I pulled off from my store.

Phoenix 'Malice' Bailey

*A*fter I dropped my t-shirt order off to Kam's Tees, I headed to class. Rich Cutz was the name of my brand that I was trying to build. I had already trademarked the name so no one else could use the shit while I was trying to get my shit up and running. I was low key pissed that I coughed up fifteen hundred dollars for fifty shirts, but she was good at what she does. I read her reviews on the internet and figured that she was the best place to go to. Her little stuck-up ass was pretty as hell, and I bet that she would probably be even prettier if she took that damn makeup off her face. She wasn't video vixen thick, and she wasn't anorexic skinny. I don't know what you would call her shape.

I was in school for Business Management. I wanted to open my own barbershop one day. I'd been cutting hair for a minute in one of the duplexes that my dad owned. That's the least that he could do for me, since he barely did shit else for me. When I was young, I had to do a lot of shit on my own. You would think that with my dad being a kingpin, I would have it all, but nah. Since I ain't want to live my life that way, he ain't want to do shit. He literally did the bare minimum, while my older brother, Pryor, or Mayhem, got all the perks of being the son of Paxton Bailey, better known as Korupt. I mean, no one would fuck with me off the strength that Korupt was my father, but at the same time, I wanted that love from my father. I needed it. My mom was pissed because of the way he treated me, but that's all she could be…pissed. She wasn't going to leave him. I mean, it's not like he treated me bad, but he treated me differently. You would think a father would want better for his kids, but nope. That nigga wanted me in the streets, as he says, to carry on his legacy.

When I was younger, I ain't take high school serious, so I ended up dropping out. When I realized that the streets were not for me, I got my GED at the age of twenty-one. After that, I did ten months in cosmetology school. Yeah, I wanted to learn how to do everything. I learned how to do more than the usual in cosmetology school because those women were breaking their necks to tutor me *privately*, especially once they found out that I wasn't gay, and I just loved to cut hair and other shit like that. I'm not going to promise that I'll be doing sew-ins all day long, if at all, but those three or four heads a week might bring in extra money.

After I finished cosmetology school, I went to the community college and took up business and entrepreneurship, and did two years with that. So, I have my Associate's degree, but I'm in school now to get this damn Bachelor's, but the shit is hard as fuck. I could only take a couple of classes at a time because the shit was expensive, and in between studying, cutting hair, and trying to make more money, the shit is stressful, but I plan to get through it because I ain't got long before school is over.

By the time class was over, I took my phone out my pocket, and had a couple of messages from niggas who wanted a cut. I texted them all back and told them to meet me at the apartment. I know that these two haircuts wouldn't take long because one of the niggas wanted a line, and the other one just wanted his afro shaped up.

I got on my motorcycle and headed to the hood. I ain't too much drive my car to the hood. I mean, I don't trust niggas at all. I don't care whose son I am, if a nigga sees some shit of yours that they want, they are going to take that risk and take it. I got one of the fastest motorcycles which is a Yamaha YZF, and it goes over a hundred fifty miles an hour, and that's pretty much my every day ride unless it rains.

Pulling up to the duplex, Spice and Retro were standing outside looking stupid. I kind of consider these niggas my friends They were down for me and everything I was trying to do with my life. Every time I was selling something, they'd always buy it, full price. We all dropped out of high school together, but the streets kept them while I let it go.

"Damn, bitch ass nigga! When the hell you get this damn bike? I know this ain't the same bike from last time. For a nigga that ain't in the streets, you sure do have a lot of nice ass shit," Retro spoke as I let us inside of the apartment.

"Man, I ain't in the streets, and that's all you need to know, dog," I laughed. "Now, sit your ass down so I can line your bitch ass up."

I plugged everything up, put on my cape, and started on Retro's line. I swear this shit came so natural to me. This is what I was supposed to do in my life. I swear I was the fastest and most efficient barber in Chicago. That's why I couldn't wait to open my shop. I planned to have a chain of barber shops with the best barbers and hairstylists in the city. The males on one side, and the females on the other. A place where people could just chill, and whatever was said in there was left in there. I am a zero-tolerance person, and if mothafuckas bring that drama shit to my shop, they would automatically be banned.

"Bro, you know Mayhem's birthday party about to be lit as fuck! It's about to be hoes galore up in that bitch," Spice laughed. "You know the hoes be all on the Bailey brothers' dick!"

"Nigga, stop hating before I run these clippers down the middle of this head," I laughed.

"I ain't hating. You know I'm calling it how I see it. I'm trying to make my girl stay home because I'm trying to find a side chick. I'm going to shoot to the mall today because you know the mall going to be packed tomorrow."

"You know it," I said as I handed Spice the mirror. "That's cool?"

"Nigga, how the hell you do that shit so fast? Bro, I swear you on your fucking way. You did that shit so fast," Spice said.

"Hell yeah. I can't wait until you make it big, my nigga. Just don't forget the small people when you make it," Retro said, looking at his line in the mirror on the wall.

"I appreciate y'all, but get y'all asses out. I have to go," I urged.

"Alright, nigga! Get up with us if you come back on this side," Retro said as he dapped me up.

When they left, I cleaned up my utensils and swept the little hair off the floor. As soon as I got finished, my phone vibrated in my pocket.

Cat: Door open. Rapist.

She always liked that dumb shit, but if someone raped her ass for real, she would have them arrested. I jumped on my motorcycle and sped to her place. She stayed in one of the best spots to live in Chicago. I pulled my motorcycle in between her cars.

Reaching into my back pocket, I pulled out my ski mask and put it over my head. I crept into her house, looking for her. She was in the kitchen looking in the cabinet.

OH MY GOOODDD! WHO ARE YOU, AND HOW DID YOU GET IN MY HOUSE!" she screamed.

"Shut up, bitch, and get on your fucking knees," I growled.

She fell to her knees, pulled my dick out of my pants, and started sucking my dick like her life depended on it. I rubbed my fingers through her silky ass blond hair before getting a good grip on it and shoving my thick nine-inch monster down her throat. After she continued to gag on it, I pulled out and picked her back up to her feet by her hair. I turned her around and bent her over the sink. I slid the condom on and rammed inside of her, hard. She kept trying to push me back, but I kept going. I spread her ass cheeks wider, and went deeper inside of her.

"Stop fighting it! You know you fucking like it," I growled.

"Please stop! Please stop!" she screamed.

I pulled out and brought myself to a release inside of the condom. I hated to do this shit with her, so I tried to finish as quick as possible.

"What I tell you about doing that, Malice? You know I can't get pregnant," Cat said as she wet a paper towel and wiped herself.

"I know you can't, but it's just a habit. I'mma jump in the shower." I pulled my ski mask off and put it back in my pocket.

"Okay, I'll get you some clothes out your drawer. Are you enjoying your motorcycle?" she asked seductively.

"Yes, it's dope! Thank you. I wasn't expecting it. You don't have to buy me stuff like that, especially expensive stuff like that, and you know I can't pay you back."

"You know I'll do anything for you, Malice. I love you," she said. "You take care of me, so I'll take care of you. Always. You said that your old bike was messing up, so I just figured I would get you a new one. It's really no big deal. You know money is nothing to me."

"I know, Cat! I know!"

"Look, Eden said that she fell in love with that huge cock, and said that she wanted to schedule something for tomorrow. You okay with that? I told her that I'll call her."

"Cat, tell her she can call me and I will see what I can do."

"Alright, I'll transfer the money now," she said as I walked into the bathroom.

Moments later, my phone chimed, and I knew it was a text message from Wells Fargo. I looked at it and saw that she had transferred seven stacks into my account. It's normally two or three, so I don't know why she transferred that much into my account. While I was looking at my account, she walked into the bathroom.

"Here are your clothes, handsome! I transferred a few more dollars because I'm going to be out of town for a couple of weeks soon, and won't be here to get my weekly dose of black cock! So, I gave you extra, unless you want to come with?"

I can't wait until I'm able to call thousands of dollars, a couple of dollars. The fuck? I thought to myself.

18

"Nah, I wish! I have a couple of hard tests coming up, and I have to study. Thank you for extending the offer though."

She placed my clothes on the sink and left out of the bathroom. I jumped in the shower and stood under the hot water.

Catherine Jenson was a fifty-five-year-old white woman who I met when I was just sixteen years old. I met her when I was working at the hospital as a janitor. She was a newly widowed patient who had just had her appendix taken out. She was a nice woman, and she stayed in the hospital for a week. Over that week, we had grown close. Not close like that, but I listened to her talk. She had lost her husband a few weeks prior in a car accident, and she was lonely, while I had told her about me having to work to make the money I wanted to make. Before she was discharged, she gave me her card and told me that if I wanted to make some real money, call her.

Being sixteen and very impressionable, I called her up the very next day. She invited me over to her house and had me doing some landscaping shit around her house, like cutting grass and shit. I did that weekly, for like a month, and she was giving me a stack a week. At sixteen, a stack a week is a lot of money. One day after working in her big ass yard, I walked in the house and she was naked. Her body was banging, and at first, I turned around so she could get dressed, but she came and wrapped her arms around me. She asked me if I wanted to make more money, and I nodded my head. She told me that she hadn't ever been with a black man before, and if I fucked her, she would make it worth my while.

At first, I was tripping because I was sixteen, and this woman was forty-three. I had fucked plenty girls, but never a woman old enough to be my mom, so I was tripping like mothafucka. She turned me around and rubbed her hands up and down my sweaty chest. She undressed me and told me that I didn't have to worry. When she dropped my pants, she was amazed at how big and thick my shit was. Her mouth started to water at the sight of it. She started sucking it, and it drove me crazy. She made me cum within like five minutes and then got it back hard.

She taught me to how to fuck her, and even how to be the best pussy eater. I still wasn't no fool though; I used condoms and dental dam when I ate her pussy. I wasn't trying to get no diseases or kids. After the first time we fucked, she gave me ten thousand dollars. TEN! She told me that I was so fucking good that she had no choice but to lace my pockets like that. Cat told me that it was more money where that came from. She took me to a gala filled with rich white people, and I swear those old white women were staring at me like a piece of chicken, while their husbands were there.

After that one night at the gala, five women called me and wanted to 'try' black dick, paying me between two and five thousand dollars every time we fucked.. It depended on what they wanted me to do. Cat never asked me for a dime of the money that I made from those women, which was skeptical to me, but if she didn't ask, then I wasn't going to say nothing.

Now, here I am, twelve years later, and I am still fucking with Cat, and I have ten loyal clients. That doesn't mean that I don't fuck more women than that, but those are the ten that I have on the appointment books for certain times and certain days. They are all married, so they don't get out of pocket and call all day. However, one of them tried to leave her husband, and I had to let her know that it ain't shit like she thinks. I'm only doing this for the money, and I'm not in love with her. After what I have been through for the last twelve years, I don't think I could ever love anyone.

The only person that knew what I did to get money was Mayhem. Of course, he told me that I didn't have to do that, and he would give me the money, but how could I appreciate something if I didn't work hard to get it myself. He just continued to tell me to be careful, and if I ever needed anything to just ask him.

"Baby! You've been in here for a while! Are you okay? One of those bitches been bothering you more than usual?" Cat asked, sliding the glass door back.

"I'm fine! Just a little tired, that's all," I replied.

"Alright, sorry for interrupting."

She closed the door, and I finished washing off. I got out and put my clothes on. When I walked out, Cat was sitting on the bed sipping some wine.

"Are you staying tonight?"

"Nah, I'm going to catch a movie and then head home."

"Can I come?" she asked.

I raised an eyebrow at her because over the decade we'd been fucking with each other, she ain't never asked me to go somewhere with me. She only invited me places with her. I'm assuming she saw my confused look, so she spoke again.

"I'm just playing. The look on your face said it all." She laughed as she sipped the last of her wine.

"Come here," I ordered.

I gave her a hug, and her short self buried her head into my chest and took a deep breath. She was acting strange, so I left quickly before this conversation went to where I was hoping that it would never go.

I jumped on my bike and headed towards the movie theater. The one thing I liked about this movie theater was that it had love seats in it. You could get comfortable and didn't have to share an armrest with nobody. The recliner seats were cool. I bought my ticket for this movie a week ago, and I bought two tickets at the same time so I wouldn't have to share with nobody.

As usual, the movie theater was packed. I didn't care what day or time you came here, it was packed. I grabbed my popcorn and a large juice, and went to my seat. I had to sit up top so I could watch both exits because you know niggas crazy these days and want to shoot shit up. I let both seats back, and was sitting diagonally on the seat, waiting for the movie to start. I was putting my phone on silent when I saw a shadow standing over me. I looked up and saw lil' mama from the store earlier staring at the number on the seat.

"The fuck you looking at?" I whispered, trying not to start a scene.

"Your legs are in my seat," she whispered back.

"Nah, I bought two seats. Move around."

"No, you bought *one* seat," she said, and tried to move my legs from the seat, but her little weak ass couldn't move me at all.

I waved her off and continued to eat my popcorn. She sat on the seat anyway, and crossed her legs over mine. She showed me her ticket, and sure enough, it was the seat she was sitting in. I grabbed my phone again to find the receipt, and sure enough, I had only purchased one ticket.

"Fuck," I whispered to myself, and snatched my legs from under her.

She looked at me and rolled her eyes like she did the whole time I was in her store.

"You should be making my shit, and you wouldn't have to fight me over my seat," I whispered to her.

"Shh." She shushed me aggressively.

I sat back against my seat and started watching the movie. At certain points of the movie, I would cut my eyes at her, and she had very dark eyes, with a very, very, very bright smile and straight white teeth. She was absolutely beautiful. Her big natural ass hair made me want to just lean in and smell it. One time I cut my eyes at her, and I could tell that she was cutting her eyes at me. I didn't look at her again after that, until I saw that she had rested her head against her fist and fell asleep. I nudged her, and she jumped awake.

"Um, if you sleepy, then you should have stayed home and let me kept my damn seat," I whispered to her.

"Shut up," she whispered back, while she stared at the screen.

Twenty minutes before the movie was ending, she had leaned

over on my shoulder. She had to be sleep again, but this time, I didn't wake her. I put my nose in her hair, and it smelled like berries and fucking coconut oil. I slightly rubbed my hands through her hair, and all of it was real. I don't know why that shit just turned me on, but it did.

The movie ended, and I'm assuming the people clapping woke her up. She jumped up again, looked at me again, and then my white t-shirt that she had gotten makeup all over it.

"I'm so, so, so, sorry," she said, gathered her things, and shot downstairs before I could catch her.

I had to wait because the stairs were packed, and when I finally made it to the lobby, she was like a ghost. I don't know why she ran away like I don't know where the fuck she worked. All I wanted to tell her was that she owed me for my fucking white Versace t-shirt that cost over five hundred dollars.

Catherine 'Cat' Jenson

$\mathcal{O}$ver the years, Malice has continuously fucked me good. All it took was one time to show him what I liked, and he took it from there. We upped it and started role-playing a lot. I could tell that he didn't really like it, but he would do whatever to please me, since I had been taking care of him literally in all ways since he was sixteen. When I first met him, he was fine as hell, and time only improved his looks. I know I was a piece of shit for coming on to a sixteen-year-old, but you ain't see what I saw between his legs one day. I mean, I only stayed in the hospital one week, but every time he walked in the room, I zeroed in on his crotch, and it was big. I got a better look at it when he thought I was sleep and he stretched. His cock was thick, and it was sitting on his thigh. Thickness, and a curve. I had to have him. I had to try black cock one time before I died, and what did I do that for?

I had always heard the statement, *once you go black, you never go back*, and that was the truth. The absolute truth. I knew it was true because my husband had a black mistress, and after he started fucking with her, he barely touched me. See, I didn't understand the power of black sex then, so I killed them both. Yeah, I know. I know. I was wrong, but he was wrong for cheating on me when I had done nothing wrong.

At first, they were meeting at a hotel every other day, and then he would stay gone for days at a time, talking about he had business meetings out of town. We did the same damn thing, worked in the same building; how the fuck could he try to get over on me about some damn business meetings out of town? Well, I followed their asses one night, and they were having a nice dinner in a secluded restaurant. I got my ass out there and unscrewed the bolts on his back tire, and they had a car accident…and died.

The sympathy that poured in after finding Brett and his mistress's body came in abundance. They never even suspected that his loving wife of twenty years could do such a thing. I sold my grief well because after he died, I sold our law firm to the highest bidder. Now, I mentor some paralegals a few nights a week at the same law firm that I sold, but they changed the name now.

Now, back to that black dick! Had I known what good black sex was back then when Brett was cheating on me with his black mistress, I would have let him keep her. I watched Malice grow from a teenage boy to a young man, and I honestly shouldn't have fallen in love with him, but I did. I was praying that once he finishes school and get his barbershop up and running, we could actually be together. I know I'm not too old have kids because I keep myself in shape, and, I just read that a sixty something year old woman carried a baby for her daughter.

I could have easily 'pimped' him out to my friends, but I didn't. I let him make his own decisions and keep all the money that he had been making from them broads. After we get together, he's going to stop fucking around with them, and if those bitches don't understand,

I can unscrew some more tires. Outside of the women he gets paid to fuck, I don't think he's been fucking with other women. I asked him one time, and he claimed that he didn't have time.

I was seriously missing him, so I decided to text him. I know that the movie was over because it's been a few hours.

Me: Hey, baby! Are you home?"

Malice: Yeah, just made it not too long ago. About to crash in a minute. I have had a long day.

Me: You want to sleep alone?

Malice: Yes. I'm tired, Cat. I'll come see you tomorrow.

Me: Okay, goodnight. I love you, Malice.

Malice: Night.

I felt stupid like I always do when he completely ignores me when I say that. I'd been telling him that for the last two years, and he's never said it back. I'm going to play it cool, because I know it's only a matter of time before we are together.

Kambridge

$\mathcal{M}$y work phone started ringing in my dream, only for me to wake up and find that it was ringing in real life. It was an iPhone, but it rang differently than my other one. I snatched it off my nightstand and cleared my throat before sliding the cursor to answer the phone.

"Kam's Tees," I answered.

"Today a holiday or some'? Maybe I'm tweakin'. I don't know," a voice said into the phone.

I knew who it was because he is never not with an attitude. I wondered why he was calling my phone so early because the store doesn't open for another two hours.

"I'm sorry?" I asked, sounding confused.

"Your fucking store opens at nine in the fucking morning, and here it is, thirty minutes after nine, and this door is locked. The fuck is you doing?"

I scrunched my nose up at his unruly attitude. I grabbed my other phone off the nightstand and looked at the time.

"Oh, crap. I'm sorry. I'll be right there. I overslept."

"Oh, no! Take your time, Prep School. The world is yours, I'm just living in it," he said sarcastically.

I took a deep breath to talk shit to him, but he had hung up before I could even get the first word out. I was so frustrated that I had overslept. I usually put myself on a pretty strict schedule, and when one thing is fucked up in that schedule, that fucks up my whole day. I walked into my bathroom and turned the shower on, while I brushed my teeth and washed my face. I stared at my bare face and wanted to cry. Not because I was chocolate, I loved being chocolate, but because I had several acne scars that I constantly covered up with makeup. People always wondered how I got so good with makeup…that's why. I didn't want to show my acne scars and get ridiculed for it. It has always been an insecurity of mine, along with the scars over my body. I probably wouldn't even have the scars it if wasn't for my father, but we won't talk about that right now.

After I got out of the shower, I sprayed my hair with some oils that I put together, and some water so it wouldn't look dry. I didn't have time to do a full beat down to my face, so I had to settle for some heavily tinted BB cream, eyelash strips, and some lip stick. I could easily do my eyebrows while stuck in some of the traffic. I'd been doing my makeup so long, I could easily do this shit in my sleep. I was just grabbing my keys when my work phone rang again.

"Kam's Tees," I answered.

"Do you know the difference between sarcasm and⌧"

"I'm on the way," I said, and hung up the phone.

Just from interacting with him over the last couple of days, I knew he was looking at the phone like '*I know prep school ain't hang up in my face.*'

29

While I was in traffic, I painted my eyebrows on. Including traffic, I made it to my store an hour later. I knew he was about to blow his top. He was leaning against the door of my store. He was in full motorcycle gear, so I assumed that the motorcycle belonged to him. I took a deep breath before I stepped out of the car. Trying not to laugh, I pulled my bottom lip in my mouth. Walking up to the door, I knew he was getting ready to say something smart.

"Nice of you to show up. I've been waiting on you for over an hour. If that is how you do business, then maybe I can get my fuckin' money back, and you can keep those funky ass jerseys."

Ignoring him, I pushed the key into the lock, pushed the door open, and turned the alarm off.

"I don't even see how you overslept when you fell asleep on my fucking shirt last night and fucked it up with all that bozo shit you got on your face."

"Does every sentence that comes out of your mouth have to include a curse word, or three, or five?" I asked as I flipped the lights on in the store.

"Hell fucking yes, it fucking do," he replied.

I didn't even reply to that. I walked to the back, put his boxes on the cart, and rolled it out to him. I pulled one out of the box to see if he approved of it. I laid it out on the counter, and his face lit up like he liked it.

"I don't like it," he smirked.

"Yes you do. You can't tell me that you don't like it. Your face lit up like a light when you saw them."

"Alright, you got me. I like them, but just a little," he admitted.

"Listen, I notice that you are on that bike, so how are you going to get these shirts away from here?"

"Hmm, that's a good question. I'll get them later."

"Oh, hell no you're not. I put you in front of other people so that I could have these jerseys done. You said that you wanted them by this morning, so you are going to take these shirts now," I snapped.

"My bad, Prep School. Give me a minute."

He stepped outside and put the phone to his ear. I was assuming he was calling someone to pick up the shirts. While he was outside on the phone, I went through my inventory to see what I needed to order. I liked to keep a lot of shit in stock because ordering only when people came in my store would knock me right out of business. A lot of the customers I got were people like Malice who need something within two or three days.

I looked up when the door chime went off, and it was Malice coming through the door. He took the boxes off the counter, and took them outside to someone waiting in a truck. He walked back in the store and stood there looking stupid.

"How can I help you, now?" I asked.

"You ruined my shirt last night when you fell asleep on it. I need you to run me them bills, Prep School."

"I can get the makeup out. Just bring it to me whenever you get a chance. Have a good day, Malice."

"Don't be trying to shut me up. If you try to shut me up, I'll just keep right on talking," he said.

Before I could reply, the door chimed, and it was my friend, Shelby Jean Long, but I call her Shelly, while her family calls her Shelby Jean. Shelly is a skinny little white girl, who lives and breathes trouble. Her family is wealthy… not rich…wealthy. There is a difference. My family is rich, hers is wealthy. She is a trust fund baby who has enough money to the point where she ain't never got to work if she doesn't want to. So, guess what? She doesn't. If only I was so fortunate.

"I'll be seeing you, Prep School," Malice said before looking Shelly up and down, and then brushing past her and out the door.

God, I hope not, I thought to myself as we made eye contact one more time before he pulled off on his bike.

"Girl, you know who that was?" Shelly asked as she twirled her long blond hair.

"Yes, a pain in my damn ass for the last two days. That's who. Where the hell you been for the last two days? I been calling you and texting you."

"Girl, in fucking jail for nothing basically," she replied.

"You don't go to jail for nothing, girl."

"Sometimes you do."

I ain't say nothing else, but I knew she was lying. Seriously, knowing Shelly, it ain't no telling why she went to jail.

"Anyways, there is a party tonight thrown by Mayhem, Malice's brother. The one who just left out of here. Everybody knows who they are. They both rolling in dough, and I just need to get close to Mayhem.

He's so fine, and Malice is just a spitting image of him. It's Mayhem's birthday, and I just want to get some of his dick. I heard it's the best. I tried to talk to him one time, but he turned me down, talking about I'm too young for him."

"Girl, you know I can't go to no parties, especially on that side of town. My dad would kill me."

"I know. That's why you are going to sneak out. I won't keep you out long. Everybody who is somebody will be there. Maybe you can find you another man and drop that stuck up ass Connor."

"Shelly, don't start. He's not stuck up. He just doesn't like you, and you don't like him, so there's that."

"Look, we are going to that party, and we are going to have fun. I swear, we will only stay until one. We will be in and out. It will be so quick, he won't even realize you snuck out. Promise," she said holding up her right hand.

After thinking about for a minute, I finally agreed to her terms. The only real trouble I'd ever been in was when I was with Shelly. Always. That was part of the reason why my dad didn't like me to hang around her. I had a couple other friends, but we weren't as close as Shelly and I were. Shelly is more down to earth than my other friends. People call me stuck-up, but if they were around my other friends, they would look at me differently.

Later that night...

It was 11:30 when Shelly texted me and told me that she was outside. I had already made my rounds in the house to make sure everyone was sleeping. My mom was in her room knocked out, and my dad was in his man cave knocked out. It was Friday night, so he indulged in several drinks. I walked past my fifteen-year-old sister, Kalena's room, and she was sleeping. I walked past Kade's room, and he wasn't in there. He was twenty-seven, so he could come and go as he pleased, and be on whatever side of town he wanted to be on. I hated the double standard.

Since my dad was passed out, I knew that it was a chance that he had forgot to set the alarm on the house. Him and Kade were the only two people with the passcode, and he does it to keep the chain on me. Also, since Kade was not here, the alarm wouldn't be set because he would set it when he came in. I'm sure that I would be back in before he does, so I felt better about sneaking out.

I had on a black sequin dress from this boutique across the street from my store, paired with my black crystalized satin t-strap heels from Jimmy Choo. See, one thing about me, you can give me a shirt that cost thirty bucks, and a pair of jeans that cost fifty, and I'll pair it with some shoes that cost over a thousand bucks, and people will think the outfit cost a pretty penny. It's all about the shoes. I love shoes. I have a whole side of my walk-in closet dedicated to shoes.

After I slipped out the door, I walked quickly to Shelly's car. I noticed that she was dressed super casual. Casual like jeans and a very low-cut t-shirt. I immediately felt overdressed.

"Look at you, hot mama. Where you think you going dressed like you ready for a fashion show? You do know where we going, right?" she asked.

"Um, I thought you said we were going to a party? Don't people dress up for parties?"

"Yeah, for the type of parties that you go to. You're dressed like a house wife going to a charity event. The bitches in this party is going to have their ass and titties out," she laughed.

I rolled my eyes because I thought that I looked nice. Forget what Shelly was talking about. We rode in silence for about thirty minutes. You could easily tell the difference in parts of the city only by driving for thirty minutes. My stomach was churning, knowing that my dad would kill me if he knew I was over here.

"Look, Kam, don't be in here acting all stuck-up. These girls in here will smell the fear on you, and pounce on you like a dog. They'll beat you up and take your damn two-thousand dollar shoes. Just play it cool, please. Don't make eye contact with nobody. Girl, just look at the damn floor when you walk in," she chuckled.

She was laughing, but I ain't see anything funny. I'm not stuck-up, and I hated when people called me that. It's not my fault that my dad forbade me to come on this side of town like my deceased grandparents didn't raise him on this side.

We parked and got out. The line wasn't long at all, and I was thankful because I didn't feel comfortable standing outside in the open. Walking in the club, the very strong smell of weed hit me in my damn face so hard that if it was a person, it would have knocked me back out the door. It was packed in here, and it was pretty much wall to wall. I was looking around like I would see someone that I knew. Shelly and I found a place on the wall to chill and people watch. Her song came on, and she left me on the wall looking stupid. She was out there shaking her backbone so hard. She ain't have no ass, so it was funny, but she was fitting in perfectly. No one even batted an eye at her. It was like everyone knew who she was already.

While Shelly continued to dance, I kept looking around. I looked up to the VIP sections and spotted Malice. I'm sure he couldn't see me because of the broad that was sitting on his lap, bouncing her shapely ass on him. He had on his jersey that he claimed he only liked a little, which made me smile a little.

"You ain't from roun' here, are you!" a girl yelled in my ear over the music.

She scared me a little because I didn't even see anyone approach me at first. I could tell she had been drinking because her breath reeked of alcohol.

"Is it that obvious?" I asked.

"Yeah, girl. You stick out like a sore thumb around here. Oh, I saw you staring up at the Bailey Brothers. I wouldn't even chance it. Those niggas are only about business, and business only. They will fuck you and leave you heartbroken. Take it from me," she said, and walked away before I could tell her that I wasn't worried about Malice nor his brother.

I looked up again, and he was gone from that spot, which was good, so now I could stop staring up there like he would actually notice me. I kept looking at the time because it was getting later and later. I kept looking around for Shelly, but she was nowhere to be found. I was starting to get frustrated…very frustrated.

Scanning the crowd, I was still looking for Shelly. My breath started quickening when I noticed that Malice was walking towards me. The jersey was wide open, displaying his rock hard tatted up body. His white jeans sat on his waist, showing off his v-cut. I could see the handle of his gun sticking out of the front pocket of his jeans. As he got closer, I prayed that he would walk right by me, but as luck would have it, he didn't.

"Looks like you on the wrong side of town, Preppy," he leaned down and spoke in my ear.

His warm breath against my ear made the hairs on my skin stand up.

"I'm on the right side of town, Mr. I kinda like the jerseys," I said, rolling my eyes while grinning like a little school girl at the same time.

"I sold them all. I'mma need some more, but not right now. How you hear about this party?" he asked.

"Um, my friend, Shelly," I said, while looking around him trying to see if I could spot her.

"Oh, that lil' white chick getting ran through now. You're going to be waiting for a minute," he said.

I guess he could tell by the look of confusion on my face that I didn't know what 'getting ran through' meant. He started laughing… laughing from a healthy place at that.

"What the hell were you learning at that school? Your ass should have gone to public school. Getting ran through means she's getting fucked by a few dudes. Listen, if you ready to go, I can take you home."

I literally gagged at the thought of Shelly fucking different men. Nasty as it may sound, I honestly wouldn't put it past her. I struggled with the idea of letting him take me home. I mean, my father is the judge, and he does lock up people like him and his friends. I don't want this to come back on us.

"Um, you should really stop wearing your emotions on your face, because I can tell that you think I'm on some type of sucka shit, but I ain't shit like that. Now, if you want me to take you home then I will."

I finally gave in and told him I would let him take me home. He told me to stay right there while he went talked to his boys. I sent Shelly a text and let her know that I was on my way home. I followed him out back and around the club. My heart started beating fast a hell.

"Um, I'm not riding on that motorcycle," I said.

"Who said you had to?" he replied as he hit the alarm on a sexy ass black Mercedes AMG. I knew what kind of car it was because it was going to be my next car. The car that I was going to buy myself when I turned twenty-five. I planned to pay cash money for it, too.

In the distance, I could hear moans, and I squinted my eyes as I glared in the semi-dark corner. Just like Malice said, Shelly was getting fucked by two dudes at the same time, and one was waiting his turn. I felt sick to my stomach. I was getting ready to go say something until Malice stopped me.

"Mind yo' business, Prep School. That ain't got shit to do with you. If she wanna be a set-out, then let her," Malice snapped.

I got in his car and then slammed the door with an attitude. He got in and stared at me. He lifted his right eyebrow at me like he wanted to say something to me, but he just shook his head. He took his gun out his pocket and put it on the armrest.

"Where you live at, shorty?"

"Lake View."

For part of the way, he was being real quiet, and every so often, I was looking at him through my peripheral, watching his chest go up and down. When he realized that the conversation was about to be non-existent, he turned the music up. It was some old-school jams, which was my type of music. At the same time, we started singing "Love Like This" by Faith Evans. I looked at him while we kept bobbing our heads to the song. He smiled, and under the street lights, I could tell that he had a pair of straight teeth.

After we arrived in my neighborhood, I told him where to go. He pulled up in front of my house, and my heart nearly hit my feet when I saw my dad sitting on the porch. He was sitting on the swing, and swinging. It was a good thing that Malice couldn't see his face, but just the silhouette of him. The time on Malice's dashboard said almost three in the morning. I smelled like weed, and I'm sure that he was going to think that I had been smoking.

"Damn, shorty, is you about to get a beat down or something? Ya old man sitting on the porch waiting for you like you snuck out the house or something," Malice joked, but I was in no mood for joking.

"Thank you for the ride home," I whispered.

"Prep School, you aight?" he asked.

"Yes, it'll be fine," I said to him, but I was staring out the window.

I opened the door and got out slowly. I knew the longer I stalled, the worse it was going to be. Malice slowly pulled off. Before my feet could even hit the top step, my dad's hand landed across my face. I rubbed where it was stinging.

"Where have you been, Kambridge?" he boomed. "You smell like weed. You been smoking? So, my rules don't matter, huh? Since, my rules don't matter⊠"

"Your rules do matter," I cut him off.

SMACK!

He backhanded me.

"Don't you cut me off when I'm talking. Since you acting like you don't have rules, I'mma show you about breaking my fucking rules."

He whipped the belt from around his waist and started hitting me with it. He kicked me in my legs, making me fall and bust my knees. I kept trying to block the licks, but they were coming faster than I could block. I just curled up against the door while the belt met with my stinging flesh. Somewhere in between the belt buckle hitting my face and body, I passed out.

Judge Kason Lewis

I sat in my office downstairs and stared at the baby picture of Kambridge on my desk. She was such a beautiful baby, and I hated that I took so much of my anger out on her, when I should have been taking it out on the right person. Kambridge was a bright and beautiful young woman. She excelled from grade school all the way through college. She opened her store without my help, nor my name. She was just a great girl, but I hated her. She was a constant reminder of a fuck up that I would probably never get over, no matter how much I told my wife that I was over it.

Before she got pregnant with Kambridge, we were having some rocky times. I was trying to become the judge, and was spending less and less time at home. She kept trying to let me know how she felt, but I was shrugging her off. She cheated on me and got pregnant. I knew almost immediately that the baby wasn't mine because we were barely having sex, and the times just didn't match up. It was a good thing that Kam looked like her grandmother on her mom's side, or I would have been really pissed that I had to look at that nigga's face all day, every day. That stupid shit doesn't excuse the way I abused her, but after all this time, I was still so pissed off. So any little thing she did, I unleashed the anger on her.

Yes, it sounds stupid that after twenty-two years I'm still pissed, but not only did Tracey cheat AND get pregnant… she cheated and had a baby from one of my biggest enemies. From my old life, I only have two enemies, and Tracey slept with one of them. Trent Wilson. That is his name. One of the biggest drug dealers in Chicago. She slept with him. If that had gotten out, that could have easily ruined my race for judge. He was one of the first people that I sent to jail for LIFE. I wasn't about to have him walking around the city mocking me. He even mocked me in the courtroom when he was escorted out.

He was standing before me waiting for his sentence for being pulled over with five kilos of cocaine, and over twenty-five thousand dollars in cash in his trunk. I knew Trent, or Big Will as the streets called him, like the back of my hand. He was very predictable, but no one would bother him because he had the police that worked that area in his pocket, but I was on some hoe shit and sent some other officers to pull him over. After I read him his life sentence, he started smiling and then winked at me. His last words have haunted me forever. *That's cool, Judge Lewis, you can lock me up for life, but no matter what you do, we will be tied together for the rest of our lives. Remember that. What's done in the dark will come to light.* After he said that, he laughed maniacally and was escorted out.

BOOM!

The door to my office opened, and in walked a steaming mad Tracey. If her skin tone was lighter, I'm sure her face would be red as hell.

"You son of a bitch," she spoke through gritted teeth. "I saw what you did to Kam, and if you put your hands on MY daughter again, I swear to God, I will divorce you in a fucking heartbeat and have you put in jail. She didn't do anything to deserve that, you sick bastard. I have let you get away with that shit for far too long because I loved you, and wanted to make the shit work with your ugly ass. I let you beat MY daughter because I thought eventually that you would forgive me, but I see that you haven't. Why didn't you just divorce me?"

I cringed every time she said *my daughter* like I haven't raised her from birth. I stared at her as the tears started streaming down her face. My anger started rising because I loved this woman with all my fucking heart, and she was standing before me talking about why I didn't divorce her.

"Tracey, you fucked my enemy, got pregnant, and he flaunted the shit in my face, in MY courtroom."

"THAT IS BESIDES THE FUCKING POINT! THAT WAS TWENTY-TWO YEARS AGO! TWENTY FUCKING TWO! YOU STILL HOLDING THAT OVER MY HEAD LIKE SOME CHILDISH ASS LITTLE BOY! I NEVER ASKED YOU TO STAY! NEVER! I GAVE YOU CHANCE AFTER CHANCE TO LEAVE ME. YOU STAYED! YOU! YOU HAVE BEEN TAKING IT OUT ON MY LITTLE GIRL EVERY SINCE SHE HAS BEEN BORN. THIS STOPS TODAY! DO YOU HEAR ME? TODAY!"

"Tracey, I'm sorry," I whispered. "I'm so in love with you. I seriously never cheated on you, and my heart was hurting after you did that. Still hurts, knowing that, that man was inside of you. Every time I look at Kam, it's a constant reminder that a man was inside of you, where no other man is supposed to be. I'm so sorry. I forgive you. I'll never put my hands on her again," I said.

"I'm not the one you should be apologizing to," she said, and stomped out of my office.

If I didn't get myself together, my wife was going to leave me. I was getting ready to go apologize when my office phone rung.

"Judge Lewis," I picked up the phone.

"It's me, Shaw. I have the information on that tag you asked me about. It belongs to a Phoenix Bailey. He also goes by the alias Malice. He is the son of⌧"

"Yeah, yeah, yeah, I know. Thank you, Shaw," I said and hung up the phone.

I leaned back in my office chair and started rubbing my temples. After damn near three decades, it was like my life was about to come crashing down right before my eyes. Pigs will fly before I lose everything that I worked hard for.

Malice

Class was easy today, and I was stoked as fuck because I wasn't feeling this shit today, but went because that perfect attendance came in handy at the end of the school term. My mind was simply on Kam, and wondered if she was okay or not. I mean, I ain't really know shit about her, but the way she feared her father made me wonder what the fuck he was doing to her in that house. I went by her the store the day after the party, but it had a closed sign on it. I even called her store number, and she didn't answer. I'm going to go by her store again after I leave this new appointment that I got today. I literally work through word of mouth. They get my cell number, and they call to set up an appointment. I send them questionnaires asking them to tell me about their fantasies. They also must have a recent STD check as well. Although I used condoms, I still wanted to be sure.

After they fill it out, they send it back to me, and I print it out and put it in their file. Yes, this shit gets real. I have a crate in the trunk of my car for the physical copies, and a digital copy on my phone. At the end of the day, these files protect me and my clients. This client today was on some real life freak master and submissive type shit, but luckily for her, I kept everything on hand. That was the reason why I drove my car this morning. I grabbed her file and my bag out of the trunk. I got the hotel in my name, and she would reimburse me, plus the three stacks I was charging her. She said she would be here by four, so I had a little time to get this swing hooked up, and freshened up.

After I got out of the shower, it was like ten minutes to four, so I sat down and went back over her file. She wanted to be treated like a slut, and fucked until she could barely walk. I slammed her file shut because that was going to be easy. She was fifty years old and black. This would be the first black woman that has paid me for sex. I ain't even think black women did shit like this.

Just as I heard the knock on the door, Cat was calling my phone. I ain't tell her about this woman, and I ain't have time to explain, so I silenced the phone and put it on do not disturb. I would just have to call her later.

When I opened the door, I saw a beautiful chocolate woman. Not speaking, she sauntered by me in the room. Getting a good view from the back, she had a big plump ass, and enough love handles for me to grab on.

"Tracey, you don't look like you are fifty years old. Time has been nothing but good to you," I said.

"Why thank you, Malice. You think a twenty-eight-year-old can handle all of this?" she teased.

"If you ain't think a nigga could, then you wouldn't have called me, woman. Take them mothafuckin' clothes off," I ordered. "First, you got the cash?"

"How do I know that you are going to be worth this?" she asked, pulling the money out of her bag.

"All my clients come by word of mouth. Again, if you ain't think I could live up to the hype, you wouldn't be here. Cash, please."

She handed me the money, and I placed it in my bag. I sat in the chair while she took off her clothes slowly. I watched her intensely. I reached into my bag and pulled my special made whip out, and laid it across my lap. I motioned for her to come here. I pulled my jeans down to my knees, and let my dick fall out of my boxers.

"Get it hard," I ordered.

She immediately fell her to her knees and took my dick in her mouth. Her mouth was so hot to the point where my dick immediately got hard.

SMACK!

I smacked her on the ass with the whip, and her ass moaned as she deep throated my dick. It's not every day that a bitch can deep throat my thick shit.

SMACK!

She deep throated my dick again and almost made me come up out the seat.

"Harder, baby," she looked up at me and moaned.

SMACK!

I did exactly what she asked me to do, and she was moaning so loud, the vibration from her moans made me blast off in her mouth. She sat back on her ass, wiping her mouth like she did something. I'd been doing this shit for so long that the first nut is just an energy booster for me. I yanked her up by her neck and walked her over to the swing. I safely secured her in the swing and then I got undressed. Once my dick was safely covered, I plunged inside of her.

From the first stroke, I started pounding her. For her to be fifty, she had a lot of grip on that pussy. I gripped her neck with both hands and started slamming into her like my life depended on it. She wanted a sore pussy, so that's exactly what I was going to give her.

"Ahhhhh! Malice! Malice! Ahhhh!" she screamed.

While I was biting my bottom lip, she was screaming like I was killing her, until she squirted all on my dick, but I kept going. Her body kept shaking and squirting the whole time. I pulled out and changed condoms.

"Damn! You worth every fucking penny," she whispered.

"I know. That's why we ain't done yet," I replied.

After I put on a different condom, I fucked her until I couldn't go anymore. That was just what I needed to relieve that stress.

After going round after round, I ain't leave the hotel until 6:30. Kam's store didn't close until seven, so I had to push it through town. I turned that thirty-minute drive into a fifteen-minute drive. I parked and got out. When I walked in the store, she was facing the wall on the phone, and curling the cord around her finger while tapping her foot. She had to be frustrated with whoever was on the phone.

Ding!

I rang the bell, and she held her finger up, signaling me to hold on. I stared at her back like she was crazy. She didn't even know who she was holding her finger up to. I could have been a murderer or something. She had on a white long sleeve t-shirt dress that was loose on her little body. Her logo was printed on the back of it.

"Yes, ma'am! I understand that. I specifically gave you instructions that said wash the shirts in cold water, inside out, and let them air dry," she said into the phone.

She got quiet for a second and grabbed the bridge of her nose.

"Ma'am, there is no need for threats. We are grown women. There were a set of instructions on the top and the bottom of the box. I know because I put them there," she argued.

"Alright! Here is the conclusion. Bring in the shirts that were ruined, and I will redo them. Yes, I need the old shirts. It's not that I don't believe you, but I need the shirts. Stop cursing at me. Ma'am! I'll tell you what! I'm not fixing anything, BYE!" she said and slammed the phone down. She took a deep breath and turned around. When she noticed it was me, she instantly looked annoyed.

"Something wrong with your jerseys too?" she asked feistily.

"Nah, I just came by to check on you and to make sure everything was alright since you were scared to get out of my car the other night," I said.

I analyzed her body carefully, and I knew that something was off. She had a huge Aaliyah type hair style which covered her right eye. I could see the welts and skin tearing on her neck. She could tell the way that I was staring at her that I thought something had happened to her, and she immediately got defensive, after pulling her clothes over the hidden scars.

"There is nothing wrong with me before you even ask," she snapped.

I reached for that bang that was covering her eye, and she jumped back, but I grabbed her by her wrist and pulled her closer to the counter. I moved it out the way, and I could see that her eye was bloodshot red, and it was swollen.

"Kam, what happened? Your dad did this to you?"

"Don't worry about it. Please don't. Just leave it alone," she stressed.

"Alright. Well fuck it!"

I left out the store. If she wanted to keep getting her ass beat by her dad, or whoever, then that's on her. I did my part. See, that's why I don't care about these stupid ass women now. I got in my car and burnt rubber out of the parking lot.

Kambridge

The rest of the time at work, I couldn't help but to think about why Malice cared about what my dad had done to me. The bruises had my body fucked up, and I had open wounds all over my body. Yesterday morning, my mom woke me screaming because I had blood all over my sheets. I had so many open wounds. My mom wanted to take me to the hospital, but I ain't want my dad to go to jail, so she cleaned and dressed up the wounds. She drugged me so well that all I wanted to do was sleep. I couldn't even open up my store yesterday because of the pain that I was in. I didn't want to miss out on too much more money, so I came in this morning. I just gave myself a big Aaliyah swoop, and came to work.

Just as I was getting ready to close the store, Connor walked in. He instantly brought a smile to my face. He was dressed in a tailored suit and making me want to jump on him. His job was so wishy washy, and he got off at different times. Between his job and studying for the bar, I barely saw him, so I was happy anytime I got to see him.

"Baby, what happened? You only wear your hair like that when your dad hits you," Connor asked as he moved my hair out of my face.

He was the only person that I told about my dad hitting me. Connor was my best friend and boyfriend at the same time. I would tell Shelly, but with her big mouth, she would probably let it slip it out of her mouth to other people she talked to. I confided in Connor one night after I ran away because he beat so bad for messing up during my violin recital. He said that I embarrassed him in front of his colleagues and other parents. I was only in junior high and thirteen years old. I stayed in Connor's apartment like room for two days before I finally went home. I told him that I would call the police if he hit me again, and he beat me again, telling me that 'he is the police.'

"Nothing. It's nothing," I replied.

I wanted to tell him why he did it, but then I would have to tell him that I snuck out and went to a party on the other side of town, with Shelly. To reiterate, they hate each other with a passion. I asked them both why they hate each other, and neither one of them had an answer. At first, I thought that they had fucked or something, but he said he wouldn't fuck her if someone paid him to, so I left it alone.

"Kam, I'm not going to leave it alone. Why does your dad keep doing this to you?"

"He hates me. My dad hates me," I cried into his chest.

"Well, I don't hate you. Let's go to your house so I can make you feel better. Then I can tell you about my day."

Just when I thought that he was going to make it all about me for once, bam, he adds something about him in there. I sighed before I locked up the store and headed to my car.

On the drive home, my phone rang and it was Connor. I pushed the button on my steering wheel and answered it.

"Yes, baby."

"Hey, I forgot that I had a study session tonight. I'll come over tonight when I'm done," he said into the phone.

Sighing deeply, I replied, "Whatever, Connor. Just go home. I'm going to be tired by the time you finish your *study session.*"

"Kam, don't act like that. You know I would love to spend every waking moment with you, but I'm trying to become a lawyer so I can make my own schedule. I'm really sorry. I'll make it up to you," he promised like always.

"You been making it up to me ever since you started the fucking study sessions, Connor. Whatever, bye," I said and hung up on him.

As soon as I hung up on him, he called back to back, but I ignored the calls. He sent a message telling me to answer my phone. I looked up to see the light had turned red, and I slammed on the brakes, just in time to only bump the car in front of me. I turned my emergency flashers on and put the car in park.

Looking up at the roof of my car, I screamed, "GOD, COULD THE DAY GET ANY WORSE!?"

I had a mini tantrum, kicking, screaming, and punching the fucking steering wheel. Like a river, the tears started flowing down my eyes. I took a deep breath before I leaned over and got my insurance and shit out of my glove compartment. Before I could even find everything, I heard knocking on the window.

"WAIT!" I yelled out.

Knock! Knock! Knock! They were tapping on the window again.

Turning around quickly, I yelled, "DIDN'T I TELL YOU TO

WAIT."

I immediately zipped my lips when I let the window down, and was met with a set of very toned abs. I wiped my tears away so he wouldn't see that I was crying.

"Get the fuck out the car," Malice ordered very calmly.

I was stuck because I thought that I was done with him when he walked out of my store today, but as luck would have it, here he is…at my car window.

"Here is my insurance…take a picture so you⊠"

"Kambridge, please get the fuck out of the car. Last time," he repeated himself very calmly.

I opened the door slowly, and he yanked it open the rest of the way. He yanked me out and pushed me against the car. I winced from the pain of the sores on my back.

"You are just dead set on fucking up my day, aren't you?" he growled.

"Yeah, maybe if I knew it was you, I would have revved my engine up more and pushed you into traffic," I said, snatching away from him and walking to the front of the car. "There is barely a scratch there. All you need is some touch-up⊠"

"Mothafucka, that's custom paint. They don't make touch-up paint for that color. So try a-fuckin'-gain," he snapped.

"Malice, look. You have my insurance information. Contact them and let them handle it. I need to get home. I'm tired. I want to take a hot bath and get in the bed," I said softly while looking at the ground.

"Whatever," he snapped. "You getting my shit fixed."

He stomped towards his car, got in, and sped off down the street. I got in my car and pulled over to the side of the road. I leaned my head on the steering wheel and started crying again. You ever felt like no one was there for you? That's exactly what I'm feeling like right now. Sometimes you just need to let out a good cry.

I jumped at the sound of someone knocking on my window. I looked out the window and it was Malice…again. I let the window down, and he told me to get out the car. I did what he told me to do so he wouldn't yank me again. I got out the car and started looking at the oncoming traffic. I couldn't look him in his face. His very handsome face.

"Kambridge, why you just sitting out here like your cute ass can't get robbed or something? This may be the good part of Chicago, but you can still get robbed. Look at me. You been crying?"

"Yeah, I been having a bad day. That's all," I said wiping my tears away.

"Good, I thought I made your ass cry or something. Look, get off the side of the street and go home to take your little bubble bath."

He started walking away, but I couldn't help but to ask.

"Malice," I called out to him. "Why did you come back?"

"I had forgot something at the place where I was coming from and noticed that you were on side of the road," he said, and immediately got in the car.

I got back in the car and drove off. This nigga followed me until I got home. I was surprised that he had a nice bone in his body. When I got out my car, my dad was sitting on the porch, on the swing.

What did I do now? I thought to myself.

I stepped on the porch and braced myself for the beat down, but instead, he asked me to come sit next to him. My heart was beating out of my chest because my dad was hot and cold.

"Kam…" He took my hands in his massive hands. "I'm sorry for how I've been treating you. I haven't been treating you like you were my daughter, and I am so sorry. I shouldn't have been ruining your beautiful skin the way that I have. I promise I won't ever put my hands on you again."

I didn't know how to take this apology because when I tell you that Judge Kason Lewis has never apologized for anything, he has not. To hear him apologizing now made me look at him crazy.

"Okay," I whispered.

That was seriously all I could muster out. I got up to go in the house, but he pulled me back down. I knew that he was about to start beating me.

"Look, there is something that Daddy needs you to do for him. You think you would be up for it?"

"Yes."

I can never say no to my dad. I learned from telling him no the first time. He tore my ass up. So everything he asks me now, I say yes. I don't care what it is.

"How do you know Malice Bailey?"

"Umm, he came in the store, and it's like he's been a pain in my behind ever since. Why?"

"Well, Daddy needs you to set him up for me. Not him. Well, his dad, and possibly his son, the other one. I need you to get to know him, so he can tell you what it is that his father and brother does. I know what they do, but I need it to come from their mouths, or someone close to them. They are very bad people, and I need them off the streets. Can you do that for me, baby girl? Once I have all the information. You will have to testify."

"Well, why can't you just lock them up, if he is such a bad man? Just tell the cops to lock them up," I countered.

WAP!

His hand went across my face so hard and fast. My hand went to my stinging face, which I'm sure was going to be purple or black in the morning.

"Don't question me, Kambridge. Damn. You got me breaking my fucking promise. Look, at first, I was asking you, now I'm telling you. Do *whatever* you must do to get that information. Do I make myself clear?"

I didn't like the way he said whatever, but I was definitely not going to question him about what it meant. I mean anyone with a brain would understand that he meant, if I had to fuck him, then that's what I had to do to get his father arrested.

"What about... what about Connor? What am I supposed to tell my boyfriend of ten years why I'm hanging out with the thug from across the way?"

"So, after I just smacked the fuck out of you for questioning me, you're going to do it again. Alright." He stood up and took his belt off.

He proceeded to whoop me, again.

WAP!

"You are going to do what the fuck I say, right?" he questioned.

I couldn't answer because I was busy crying, and trying to block the licks.

WAP! WAP! WAP!

"So, you ain't gon' fucking answer me, Kambridge? If you don't do it, I'll kill you. You know I'll get away with it. I'm a judge," he snapped before hitting me again.

WAP! WAP!

"YESSS!" I screamed out in pain. "I'll do it! I'll do it! I'll do it! Please stop!"

He towered over me as I laid on the swing, covering my face. He was breathing hard, and the way he watched me, I thought that he just wanted to recharge before he beat my ass again. He walked in the house, leaving me on the swing.

After ten minutes, I hobbled in the house. I peeked in Kalena's room, and she was sitting on the edge of the bed crying, like always. Kade was almost never home, but he knew what happened to me. When I was younger, he would save me, but now that he is gone a lot, no one is there to save me. My mom ignored him, and Kalena only cried.

"Kalena, I'm okay. Stop crying and go back to sleep," I whispered, as I tried to cuddle her, but the pain was too unbearable.

"Why does he always do this to you? Why is he so mean to you, Kam? I love you so much. I don't want you to die," she sobbed.

"Kalena, your big sister is going to be alright, okay? Get some rest. We will go get some ice cream tomorrow after school, okay?" I bargained.

She nodded her head and laid back down. I kissed her on her forehead several times before I crept out the room and shut her door. I hobbled in my bathroom and looked at the wounds. I cleaned them off with alcohol, and it burned so bad that I cried. I got in the shower, and cleaned myself as best as I could before the pain became unbearable.

I grabbed my Louis Vuitton huge overnight bag, and started stuffing clothes in it. I was not about to take any more of my dad's beatings. I grabbed my makeup bag, and scooped everything off the counter into it. I set my bags on the bed, and I looked through it, making sure that I had everything that was a necessity. I grabbed my keys and crept out of my room. I made sure Kade was still gone, and Kalena was still sleeping.

When I made it to the front door, I took a deep breath and left out the front door. I threw my things in the front seat and backed out. As soon as I got to the end of the yard, Kade was getting ready to pull his Ferrari in the yard. He swerved and pulled next to me and let his window down. I let my window down.

"Kam, where you going, girl? It's late. I know you ain't sneaking out for that white dude," Kade said.

I shook my head and started crying.

"Aw shit! Dad up to that shit again. Come here right quick before you go."

I got out the car, and he pulled me in for a hug. He kissed me on my forehead.

"Sis, I wish there was more I could do. I'm so sorry," he apologized. "Just call me and let me know when you get to where you going. I love you, sis. So much."

I got back in the car and pulled off. Honestly, I didn't have a destination in my mind, but I ended up on Connor's street anyway. He still stayed with his parents so he could save for law school when he gets in. I called him, but he ain't answer the phone. Pulling closer to his house, I could see him and Holly outside being very animated with their arms. You could tell that they were arguing. They were so engrossed in their argument that they ain't even see me creeping up the road. I pulled up to them and let my window down. I ain't even say shit, I just nodded my head.

"Kam, it's not what it looks like," Connor said.

"What do I think it looks like?" I asked.

"Can we talk, please?"

Connor walked to my car and tried to open the door, but it was still locked. I let the window up and burnt rubber getting away from him and his lying ass. He called my phone back to back, but I ain't answer. I blocked him from my phone all together. I'll unblock him in a few hours, when I was sure that he was done calling.

I drove for an hour and turned into the first hotel that I saw. I knew that my dad could find me if he wanted. I pray that he let me have a few days to myself before he came and dragged me away from the hotel. As soon as I made it to my room, I took some pain medication and went to sleep.

Malice

Sitting on the bed listening to Cat ramble on and on, my mind drifted to Kam. As much as me and my dad didn't get along, he had never abused me. At least that's who I think was abusing her. I had to find out more about her dad. Cat straddling my lap shook my thoughts away from Kam.

"What's wrong, baby? You seemed to be stressed out," Cat said, wrapping her arms around my neck.

"Nothing, really. You all packed, and ready to go," I asked.

"Yeah, but I can't go until you fuck me, and fuck me hard," she whispered in my ear.

She started grinding against my lap, making my dick hard as hell. I reached into my back pocket and grabbed my wallet. I pulled the gold packet out and held it between my teeth.

"Malice, why do we always have to use a condom? I want to feel you for once," she whined.

"Cat, we have already been through this. It's better to be safe than sorry. I don't want any kids right now. Maybe after I graduate or something," I lied.

I just can't get her pregnant. She is old enough to be my mom. It's weird that she even wants kids with someone when she ain't met no one in my family. Not ever. I ain't never fucked her raw, and I don't ever plan on it. If I ever find someone, she's going to be around my age, and she is going to be black. I'm just doing what I have to do until I get my own shit up and running.

"Whatever. You have been saying that for the longest," she said, getting on her knees.

She pulled my dick out and started sucking it like she was trying to suck the skin off it. She was getting it extra sloppy, and it was turning me on even more. Before I could even get my nut off, she raised up and started talking shit.

"You let me suck your dick with no condom, but you eat me with dental dam, and fuck me with a condom. Don't you think if I had anything, I would have given it to you by mouth by now, plus, you make sure I get tested every other week. Why don't you kiss me? What is the problem, Malice?"

"You can't get pregnant through your mouth. You're making my dick soft with all that politicking, to be honest. I don't know why *you all of a sudden* have a problem with the arrangements, Cat. Come on. It's been this way for twelve years. Twelve. I ain't never kissed you. I ain't never fucked you raw, nor ate your pussy without no dental dam. You trippin' for real. You just turned me off. Let me get you to the airport," I said, putting my soft dick back up.

Her face started turning red, and her eyes started watering. Slouching my shoulders, cocking my head to the side, I glared at her. I didn't mean to look disinterested, but I was. I didn't care for the crocodile tears like this was something that I just came out of my ass with. One of the main reasons I didn't kiss her or eat her pussy without the dental dam was because she smoked cigarettes. She'd been trying to hide it from me for the longest like I was stupid. Whether people know it or not, whatever you put in your body is going to come out through your skin or your secretions. Who wants liquid cigarette in their mouth? Weed is cool, but cigarettes, no.

"It's because I love you, Malice. Damn it! After twelve years, you don't feel shit for me? I know you feel something for me." She crossed her hands across her chest and started pacing the floor.

My eyes went from side to side because I was confused. I started laughing, until she dropped down to her knees and started wheezing and grabbing her chest at the same time. I stared at her because she has done this before. She does this shit to get her way, and I don't know why she does this because it has only worked one time, and it won't work again.

"Catherine, you need to get the fuck up so I can take you to the airport, so I can go visit my parents. You know I ain't none of those weak dudes that you be fucking with. You can't get your way with me. Get up," I growled.

"I don't fuck with no other men but you, Malice. Please. Just give us a chance," she begged.

"Cat, you know we got a tight bond, but I never allowed myself to open up to love anyone nor be loved because I just ain't on that right now. I'm too busy to be in any type of relationship. Cat, if it makes you happy, you are the only woman that I converse with every day."

She sat there for a minute, got up, and went to clean herself up. I grabbed her suitcase and took it to the car. I sat in the car and waited for her to come out. Moments later, she came out and got in the car, slamming my door. Women ain't never fucking satisfied, bruh. I sped to the fucking airport, just to get her out the car. A part of me was glad that she was going to be gone for the next two weeks.

∞

Pulling into my dad's estate, I had to take a couple of deep breaths before I went inside. I knew that we were going to have the same conversation before he gave me the information I asked him for. I tried to come out here as little as possible because my dad was so annoying. My mother came by the house I share with my brother so that's how I saw her when I did.

Stepping out of the car, my mom was coming around the house running. She always tried to keep in shape.

"Son! I ain't know you were coming by today. I would have cooked something for you. How are you?" she asked, pulling my tall self into her arms. "I missed you so much." She buried her head into my chest.

"Ma, I missed you too," I said, kissing her forehead.

Following her into the house, I immediately felt the negative energy.

"Where Korupt at?" I asked.

"You know he in his office, honey. Come see me before you leave, please," my mom spoke before she walked away.

I walked down the long hall to Korupt's office. I knocked on the door, but there was no answer. I seriously stood out there knocking for ten minutes before this nigga told me to come in. He had his seat turned towards the window, not even acknowledging me. I shook my head at the blatant disrespect.

"Did you get that information for me?" I asked.

I seriously hated to ask this nigga for anything, but I ain't want nobody else in my business, and I knew that he could get information on anyone.

"Yeah, I got it. What are you willing to do for it?" Korupt asked turning around in his seat.

"What the hell you mean by that? *What I'm willing to do for it?*" I mocked him.

"Malice…look, you have so much more potential than you know, to run my business with your brother. You street and book smart. You can take my business to even higher heights, and you know it. Why don't you want to get into the family business?"

"Korupt, we get into this every time I see you. THE STREETS ARE NOT FOR ME! Always having to watch your back. Can't have a regular fun life because you always on the go. Only thing in them streets is death and jail, and I ain't trying to see either one of them soon. It's already enough being your son, but to actually get in the *family* business. Nah. I just can't. I want a regular nine-to-five job."

"You'll make more money in the streets than slanging that Bailey dick. Oh, don't look surprised, son. You know I know everything that happens in this city. Can't nothing slip by me."

"It has paid for me to go to school and everything I have now.

66

More than you have done. Look, do you have the information or not, since you know everything that happens in this city?"

He pulled a file from his desk, and held it up between his fingers.

"Yeah, I have it. There wasn't nothing too much to look into. I actually have some unfinished business with the father of this broad, which is the only reason why I'm doing this for you. You have to do something for me," he smirked.

"I knew it. You said okay too damn fast when I called you and asked you to do it." I waved him off. "Never mind."

"Years ago, before you were even born, her father took something from me and I want it back. I know that he has it. Get in good with her so she can give you the information."

"What does he have of yours that you just can't ask for it back, or just...*make* him tell you, like you do everyone else."

"It's not that easy. Her dad is a judge. Judge Kason Lewis. It will be hard to get to him. He ain't always been a judge, so I won't be able to *make* him tell me anything. Her dad stole my gold. Today that gold is worth two million, two hundred fifty thousand. I want it back. I know he has it," he assured me.

"How you know he has it?"

"He is the only person who knew I had it. Just do like I ask. If you get me the right information, then I'll never ask you to join the family business again. I will make it bearable for you to be around me and buy your little barbershop."

"Wait, I have to do something for you... for you to treat me like your son… and do shit that a father is *supposed* to do for his seed? Wow! That's a new low for you, but anything for you to leave me alone about them streets."

"Don't be dramatic, Malice. I'll do anything for you. All you have to do is ask. That's *you* who be trying to be so high and mighty like you don't need me or my bills. You don't ask… I won't do. Point. Blank. Period. You need me, and I need you. Right now, I *need* you to help me get my gold back. That's it for now."

I ignored him and tried to snatch the file from him, but he moved it back quickly.

"Her name is Kambridge Lewis, which you already know. You already know where she works, lives, and who her dad is. Pretty much all you need to know about her. The rest of the stuff you have to find out on your own because if you know everything, you won't listen when she tells you about herself, and you'll run her away before you can find out where my shit is. Now, leave me to my work. I'll be checking in with you in a couple of weeks."

"A couple of weeks? How you expect her to just tell me some shit like that in two weeks? She don't know me, and I don't know her like that."

"You're a Bailey," he responded before he picked up his ringing cell phone.

I sat there stunned at the task he just gave me. I ain't never used anyone for anything, and for him to ask me to do that just to have a real relationship with him, had my head spinning. I continued to stare at him, while he was speaking into the phone like he had two heads on his shoulders.

"You need anything else?" he put the speaker of the phone into his shoulder and asked me.

I shook my head no, and he shooed me out of his office. I left the house, not even telling my mom bye like she wanted me to. I sat in my car for a minute before I backed out of his house. This was going to be weird because me and her were COMPLETE opposites.

Pryor 'Korupt' Bailey

I was not messed up about giving my son that task to do, because if he don't do shit else for me, he can do that. See, Malice thinks that I don't love him or I treat Mayhem different, but that's false. I love both of my sons the same, and on the outside looking in, a person would think that I treat Mayhem different, but it's because we have more in common and we work together. Mayhem is the head of operations for my business, so of course we have a closer relationship. I will do anything for Malice that he wants, but he claims every time he asked me to do something for him, it always came with a stipulation. That is true, but damn! I needed my son to see that the streets was where he needed to be. So, he stopped asking me for shit and I stopped giving.

Honestly, I always knew that Malice would be different. When the boys were younger, Mayhem wanted to know about guns, and Malice read books. I started taking Mayhem to the gun range when he was eleven. When Malice turned eleven, he didn't want to go. The few times he did go was because his brother begged him to go. I'm proud of my son because he did something no one in my family has done, and that's completed high school and got their GED. It took him a minute to do it, but he did it. Then he's in college getting his degree. I can't hate on that, but I wanted him in the Bailey family business. I tried to make him understand that him not being in the game doesn't make him less of a target, because his last name is Bailey.

The family business is a taxi company. I own a taxi company, and that is how my drugs are distributed throughout the city. Simple. Instead of my soldiers standing on corners or working in trap houses, they drove taxi cabs. It's so easy to blend in with the streets doing that. All I needed Malice to do was to run the books, making sure that everyone was getting everything they needed and that the money was never off. In a sense, he wouldn't be getting dirty, but you know eventually, he would have to.

As soon as I put my phone down, it rung again, and it was my boy Big Will, also known as Trent Wilson. This nigga is my right-hand man, even from that cell. My nigga been in that bitch for twenty-two years. Twenty-fucking-two.

"What up, fam?" I answered the phone.

"Nigga, same shit, same toilet, just a different day. What's good?"

"Mane, not shit. Just holding down the fort until you bring your black ass home."

At this point, we both know he was going to die behind those bars, but I did whatever I could to help him keep his head up.

"My nigga. One day. What's new?"

"You wouldn't even believe what Malice asked me for?"

"You still treating my godson like shit? I don' told you about that shit, fam. Let him do what he does. If he tells you the streets not for him, then believe him. Those be the first ones that get that scalp peeled back, and I'd be pissed if a nigga laid my godson down and I couldn't get to 'em. Leave him alone, Korupt."

"I don't treat him like shit, but I hope you done preaching. So, he hit me up asking for information on Kason and Kambridge. He met her at her store, and then he saw her again at Mayhem's party. He dropped her off at their home, saw her father sitting on the porch like he was waiting for her, and the next time he saw her, she had bruises on her face and on her body."

That nigga got quiet as fuck on the phone. It was like I could hear him squeezing the phone.

"I should have been bagged that nigga when I had the chance. He putting his hands on my fucking daughter. Man, she need to know who her real father is, and soon. I want to get to know my baby before he kills her, and I have to break out this bitch and murk him. I mean that shit," he snapped.

"I know, bro! I know! Well, I told him to get to know her, so⊠"

"You telling your son to fuck my daughter?"

"Hell no, nigga, but if it comes down to it, he got to do what he has to do. I just want my shit back that I know that her bitch ass dad has."

"Bro, you still worried about that fucking gold. Had you told me to begin with, we wouldn't have even been going through this shit right now. Can't believe you trusted that geek over me."

"Man, chill. You know what it is. Young and dumb back then. I never thought for one second that he would switch up the way he did, but it's aight; his time coming. Once I get my shit back, it's lights out for that nigga."

"Alright, fam. I'm about to go get something to eat. I'll holla at you later," Big Will said and hung up the phone.

Big Will and I'd been cool ever since we were younger. Our parents stayed right next to each other, and we also went to school together. Our fathers were small time hustlers who worked for another nigga. We may have lived in the projects, but we had the biggest apartments, and the insides were laid like a palace. They were also right hands to each other. When we were both fifteen years old, the streets claimed our dad's lives, and that's when we dropped out of school and started hustling. Our fathers did not want that for us, but hell, who was going to feed our moms?

I met Kason's bitch ass when he was walking home from school one day. Well, I had seen him around the way, but we ain't never shared nothing but a head nod from time to time. He lived in the building across from ours. Anyways, he was about to get jumped and was about to get his brand-new school shoes taken. Me and Big Will beat them niggas' asses, while his bitch ass ran home. I should have known then that he was a bitch ass nigga, but I wanted to give him the benefit of the doubt.

The next day, me and Big Will was sitting on our front steps, and I saw Kason getting out his mom's car. I called him over and introduced ourselves. He told me that he didn't have any friends and shit, so we took him in. He wasn't doing no major work, but just picking up and dropping off packages because I didn't want him to stay out late because he was smart as hell. He was the type of nigga that the streets were just not for, and I didn't want to do that to him. He was making enough to help his parents out, and keep a little lunch money in his pocket. Nothing too extravagant.

Now, fast forward to when we were a few years older. Big Will and I decided that we were ready to take our hustling to the next level. We were ready to cut the middle man out, so we got a small team together and took out our connect, Slug, when he least suspected it. While I told everyone to get away, I stayed back because Slug used to always talk about how he had some gold that he stole from his connect. I tore his house up looking for it, and after a whole twenty-four hours of looking for it, I finally found it after breaking up the cement part in his basement. When I first saw that gold, my eyes lit up like kid in a candy store. It took a minute to figure out a plan to get the gold out, but I did, and put it in a safe space.

Fast forward again, we were having Kason a graduation dinner at the house, and this nigga got drunk talking about he wanted to rob somebody, and that he was ready to take his hustling to the next level. Everybody was shocked because everybody knew Kason was a bitch. Kason said he didn't have no money for school, so he wanted to get deeper in the game. So, we pulled up to a corner store right before they were closing. I gave him my banger and told him to go in there and handle his business. This nigga went in there, pulled the gun out, and then bitched out. This BITCH ass nigga dropped my fucking gun, and ran out the fucking store. I was pissed. So, you know what happened next.

That very same night, 12 showed up to my door and arrested me right on the spot for armed robbery. I could have ratted on Kason, but

I didn't. I served my five years like the 'G' I was. During that time, I had called Kason and told him about my gold so he could move it to an even safer spot. For the life of me, I don't know why I trusted Kason over Big Will, but that was the biggest mistake of my life.

By the time I had gotten out of jail, I hadn't talked to Kason in years, and came home to find out that the nigga was in college, and paid for the shit in full. Nigga had moved his parents out the hood and all that shit. I had finally got in contact with him to ask him where my shit was, and he told me that he didn't know what I was talking about and hung up on me. For a while, I had gone on a rampage trying to find my shit, but I was unlucky as fuck. So, Kason wouldn't talk, so I paid his parents a visit. It didn't end well for them. I attended both of their funerals with a smile on my face. Kason pulled me to the side, told me that he knew I was behind it, and he wouldn't stop until I was rotting behind the walls of a jail. He also told me that if I thought for one second I was getting my gold back, then I was wrong, and he walked away from me. That was the last time I saw Kason, before he became Judge Kason Lewis, who keeps security on him everywhere he goes. Couldn't touch that nigga even if I wanted to…at least not yet. Little Miss Kambridge couldn't have come in Malice's life at a more perfect time. After I get my gold, it's lights out for that nigga. Laying Kason down is going to bring me such great joy.

Kambridge

 wo days later, I was still laying in the hotel bed. I was so sore, and it's like every time I tried to move, I couldn't. For the last two days, I hadn't done anything but lay in the bed. I hadn't eaten, taken a shower, or any of that. My phones had been ringing off the hook, but I just couldn't talk to anyone. I was sure that my dad could come get me whenever he wanted to, but I guess he called himself letting me get over this shit.

Knock! Knock!

"Room service," the voice said at the door.

The woman casually walked into my room while I was laying in the bed. She was an older black lady with her scrubs on.

"Oh, I'm sorry, I can come back," she said. "I didn't know you were in here. So sorry!"

"It's alright! I will sit in the chair. I think I need new sheets anyway," I sleepily said.

I winced at all the pain I was in as I tried to transition from the bed to the chair, but I just couldn't.

"Ma'am, are you alright? Do I need to call the ambulance?" she asked. "My name is Dorothy.

"No, I can make it. Thank you for asking. I haven't eaten in a couple days, and I just need my medications," I admitted.

That had to be the reason that I was in so much pain because I hadn't been in this much pain since the first time my dad beat me. This was the worst. I finally made it to the chair, and I was going through my phone and saw I had several text messages from my family, Connor, and Shelly, but I just didn't have time. My work phone rung, and I didn't want to answer it, but I hadn't switched the button to turn on my 'away' voicemail. I mustered up all the strength I could and answered it. I hope it wasn't a rush order because I didn't feel like having to dope up, and do shirts. The last time that happened, I fucked up fifty shirts and lost a thousand dollars.

"Kam's Tees," I answered the phone.

"How the fuck do you make money if you ain't never here?" Malice's loud voice boomed into the phone.

My heart sped up at the sound of his voice because what my dad wanted me to do had rushed back to my mind. A lump formed in my throat because I could not answer him.

"How…can," I cleared my throat. "How can I help you?"

He started talking to me, but I couldn't hear anything because I was looking at Dorothy holding up the sheets with green and red stains on them. I looked down at myself, and saw that several of my wounds had dry blood around them, along with green stuff oozing out of them.

"Sweetie, I think you should go to the hospital," she said in such a concerned voice.

"KAM! HOSPITAL! WHAT THE FUCK IS GOING ON? WHERE ARE YOU?" Malice yelled into the phone.

I mentally cursed the woman for speaking so loud that Malice's nosey ass could hear her. I slowly pressed the end button on the phone, hanging up in Malice's face. I got up as fast as the pain would allow me. I gathered my things and left out of the hotel room. I went downstairs to check out so I wouldn't get charged for an extra day. I drove myself to the nearest emergency room. When I checked in, I told them I think I had some wounds that got infected. The whole time I'm talking to the woman, Malice kept ringing my work phone. The woman told me to sit down, and that they would be with me in a few. I hoped that I wouldn't have to wait long because people were starting to stare at me since I had on a bloody and green stained white sleeping dress.

"Lewis," the nurse said from the door.

I hobbled over to her and went into the back. Once we got to the back, she introduced herself. She looked me up and down like she wanted to say something not related to work, but she kept asking me questions. She asked me to get undressed, and I froze because I hated to show my skin to anyone. The healed scars, the new scars, the old scars that became new scars again, were just a lot for anyone to see.

"Ms. Lewis, the only way we can help is if we survey all the damages," Nurse Lockett said.

I slowly pulled my sleeping dress over my head, and I could hear her gasp. I started crying because of her shocked expression.

"Kambridge? Can I call you Kambridge? Please, don't cry. I'm sorry for my reaction. I just… I'm sorry," she whispered.

The doctor came in, announced herself as Dr. Terry, and started looking at my wounds.

"Kambridge, some of these wounds are very infected. I'm surprised you still could move as much as you have. I have to drain them, and some of these needed stitches, but you didn't come in, why?"

I shrugged because there was no way that I was going to tell on my father.

"You are going to have to take antibiotics for the next week, and I'm going to give you a shot of Toradal for the pain that you are in now, and I'm not letting you walk out of here in that dress. I have some scrubs that might fit you, okay?"

I nodded my head. She left out of the room and left me in there with Nurse Lockett again.

"I know a shelter," she whispered.

"This happened at my shelter," I replied.

Before she could respond, Dr. Terry walked back in the room with her materials. For the next hour, she drained several of the infected areas and wrapped them up. She gave me a shot with a thick ass needle in my hip, and I almost cried. When she was done, she went and got me a pair of scrubs. She told me that I looked like a small, so when I put them on, they fit perfectly. She wanted me to sit in the room and wait a minute to see how my body would react to the pain shot that she gave me.

"Kambridge, if you need a place to stay, you can come live with me for a little while," Nurse Lockett offered.

"No, it's fine. I couldn't escape him no matter where I go. Thank you for offering," I whispered.

"Why can't you escape him? Who is him? We can have him arrested," she said.

Before responding, Dr. Terry came back into the room and told me that I was good to go and gave me my prescription for my medication. She left out just as quick as she came.

"Kambridge, why can't we have him arrested?" Nurse Lockett asked.

I gathered my things to leave the room. When I opened the door, I turned and looked at her and replied, "The him is my father."

I left out of the room and found the nearest bathroom. I pulled my mini makeup bag out, and started doing my makeup. I'm sorry, but I couldn't show off all this acne scarring. I should be worried about getting better, but instead, I am worried about people seeing the scarring on my face. After I was satisfied with my face, I headed out to my car. As soon as I made it outside, I saw the thorn in my ass pacing in front of my car. *Why does he keep showing up in my life?* I thought to myself.

He was smoking what looked like a blunt, and he looked good as fuck. He had on black jeans, black Timbs, and his motorcycle jacket with his last name on the back. I stopped and dipped behind another vehicle. I don't even know why I dipped because it ain't like he was going to leave until he laid eyes on me. I was trying to peek above the truck I was behind, but he was gone.

"KAMBRIDGE!" I jumped at the sound of my name.

I turned around and was faced with a steaming Malice. It was like you could see the steam coming out his ears. His cheeks were turning rosy. We stared at each other momentarily, and I took in more of his facial features. His eyes were so dark… and cold. His skin was remarkably smooth. He wasn't as dark as me, but he wasn't light skinned either. He was…red. I smirked at the thought of calling him red.

"So, you think this shit is fucking funny?" he snarled.

"Do I think what is funny?" I asked.

"You ain't hear shit I said to you?"

"No, I didn't. I'm sorry."

The minute he started talking, I became engrossed in his thick lips, but my growling stomach prompted me to wrap my arm around it, like that would stop it from growling.

"The fuck wrong with you?" he snapped.

Even when he is concerned, he has an attitude.

"I haven't eaten in two days. I'm hungry," I said.

"I know a spot. Follow me," he ordered.

"Is this a date, Mr. Malice?"

"Fuck no," he replied, before putting on his helmet and walking away from me.

I rolled my eyes at him before walking to my car and getting in. He pulled off on his motorcycle with me in tow. My dad better be glad that I want his ass whoopings to stop, or I would not waste my time getting to know his mean ass.

Malice

For the life of me, I ain't know why this girl was on my mind heavy. Maybe it was because of what my dad wanted me to do, or it was because she really needed some type of help. When I stopped by her store and it was closed, I automatically thought something was wrong. When I called her work phone and heard whoever that was in the background told her that she needed to get to the hospital and she hung up on me, I was low-key scared a little. Man, I called every fucking hospital until I finally found out where she was.

When I pulled up to the hospital, I rode around until I found her car. I pulled my bike next to her car and fired up the blunt that I had in my jacket pocket. I hadn't smoked in a minute, and I only smoked when my nerves were on ten. This girl gives me anxiety so bad. Aside from my dad's bullshit, I really wanted to help her, and she wouldn't let me. When I caught her trying to hide from me, I noticed that she had bandages on both of her arms. If I ain't know any better, I would swear she was trying to slit her wrists.

I kept looking in my mirror to make sure that she was still following me because I could tell that she can be real tricky sometimes. Fifteen minutes later, we pulled into this restaurant that served soul food. Hopefully, she eats stuff like this because she is a tiny girl. Fuck it, if she ain't eat it, she was going to eat it today because she needs some meat on her bones. I locked my helmet on the back of my motorcycle, and went and yanked her car door open.

"Does everything you do and say have to be done with so much attitude, damn," she snapped before grabbing her Celine purse out the back.

The only reason I knew it was Celine is because I bought Cat one just like it for her birthday a few years ago. So, I'm sure that she is a spoiled brat.

"Yeah, this is just the way that I am. Take it or leave it," I snapped back.

"I'll leave it."

Throwing her purse in the passenger seat, she tried to shut the door, but I grabbed it to stop her from closing it. I gave her a look that told her she better stop fucking playing with me. She grabbed her purse again and got out. We sat ourselves once we were in the restaurant, and once we placed our orders, she was looking down at the table.

"So, why would you try to kill yourself before I get a chance to?" I smirked.

"I didn't try to kill myself. If I wanted to kill myself, I would have been done that, so mind your business, ugly. Wait a minute, what was the end of that?"

"Nothing, Prep School," I laughed.

"Stop calling me that," she spoke through gritted teeth.

"Or what?" I replied, while raising my eyebrow at her.

She put her head down and started looking through her phone. When the food came, we both began to dig in silently. She was eating like she hadn't eaten in days.

"When the last time you ate? You eating like a pig eating slop."

"Uh, I told you a couple of days. I just been sleeping on and off. I was in so much pain, Malice. You just don't understand," she said as her eyes welled up in tears.

"Well, help me understand then, damn!"

"Don't get so snappy, Malice. You really do curse a lot. It's really annoying and shows that you have a lack of education," she casually said like she didn't just insult the fuck out of me.

"Kambridge, actually, people who use profanity are smarter than those who don't. Several studies have proven that. I can curse you and your mother out like a wet sailor, and teach you how to optimize business functions, and create efficient processes all in the same breath. Now, don't ever fucking try to play me," I snapped.

I pulled out my wallet and dropped a couple of twenties on the table, and walked out before she could respond. I was pissed the fuck off. I hated when bitches or anybody tried to count me out because of where I come from, the way I talk, or my tattoos. Hell, I'm in the top of my very competitive class. If I can keep it up, I will be graduating with honors, but stupid ass in the restaurant would know that if she asked and not assumed. I pulled my phone out my coat jacket and called my dad.

"Whoa! That was quick, son. I wouldn't have expected it this soon," my dad said into the phone.

"Nah, it ain't gon' work. I don't like her. She don't like me. It's not going to work. Find another way to get your shit. I'm done," I snapped.

"Son, see, it's not going to work like that. I don't care if you don't like her. You better pretend like you do for the sake of my two million dollars. Just to up the ante, I'll give you five hundred thousand of that when I get it. Now, bye."

"Da--"

He hung up the phone before I could even call his name. I took a deep breath before I walked back into the restaurant. She was still sitting there, and it looked like she was still eating. I walked over and plopped down with an attitude.

"Oh, you thought I was going to chase you? I'm hungry. Maybe if you weren't such an asshole⊠"

"You're either going to say you are sorry or you're not. Either way, I don't give a damn, Prep School." I started picking around my food. "Did you poison my damn food while I was outside?"

"Yeah, I took it to the bathroom and added some special juice. Eat up," she laughed, and in turn, making me laugh.

"Malice, I'm sorry. I was really judgmental a minute ago. I don't why⊠"

"You were taught that way. It's all good. So I guess while we sitting here, tell me how you ended up in the hospital."

"Stop trying to get in my business."

"Damn, well, tell me about yourself. Make some type of conversation."

"Well, my name is Kambridge Lewis and I'm twenty-two. My dad is a judge, and my mom is vice president of human resources. I have an older brother and a younger sister. I went to private schools all my life. I have a Bachelor's in Business and when I graduated, I opened my store. That's pretty much it. Nothing too spectacular. Oh, I play the violin," she laughed.

"Damn, you boring. What type of shit you do for fun, besides fall asleep on strangers in movie theaters? Speaking of, I need to give you my shirt."

"I travel. I have been to several countries. I want to fill my passport up before I'm twenty-five."

"Still boring and sounds like rich people shit. Only rich people play violins, and *travel to different countries*," I mocked her.

"I won't apologize for my *rich* background, Malice. Contrary to popular belief, traveling is not expensive. You don't necessarily have to travel outside of the country. You can just travel to places you've never been before. Learn different cultures, and just do shit that you have never done before. It's not about money."

Tell that to my rich father who wants me to use you to get to your father, I thought to myself. Honestly, I did feel a certain way about it because I have never traveled out of the country to be honest, and I'm twenty-eight years old. Korupt and Mayhem have, to conduct business, but of course I couldn't go. The only place I have really traveled to was Las Vegas for my twenty-first birthday. Damn, that's the only place I have ever been, and we drove there because Korupt wanted Mayhem to pick up some work from a nigga. Me, Mayhem, Retro, Spice, and

Metro, Mayhem's best friend, and Retro's older brother, drove across the fucking country so we could turn up for my birthday. Other than that, I go out the city to meet some of my clients at hotels. That's it. When I put it like that, my life was boring too, I guess.

"Don't be so concerned with making money that you forget to live your life. Money comes and goes, but you'll have experiences forever. You'll have stories forever. Trust me. When I get older, I want to be able to tell my kids, if I ever have any, all the places that I have traveled to, not me being too busy to have a life, and I end up trying to live my life through them, or be that thirty-five-year-old at the club. Self-care is very important, and my self-care is playing my violin, the movies, or traveling. What's yours?" she asked me.

Once again, she has left me stumped on something that she has said. I guess she's not a bitch after all.

"For the most part, I guess I could say smoking. Smoking is my self-care because when I get stressed, or my anxiety rises, I smoke, but that's not often."

"I was self-caring when I bumped into you at the movies. Self-caring from that episode you put on when you first burst into my store. You're really annoying, you know that?"

"Aye, we really ain't cool enough for you to just be telling me how you feel like that, Prep School."

She giggled a little, and said, "So, I stress you out? How? You don't even know me. You were smoking when I came out the hospital. You said that you only smoke when you're⊠"

"Girl, I know what I said, but yeah. I was calling you, and you weren't saying anything. The woman in the background was talking about you needed to go to the hospital and shit. I don't like you or anything like that, I just wanted to know if you were okay. It was hard trying to find someone to get my jerseys made, so of course, I don't want anything to happen to you," I laughed. "Where were you anyway?"

"You're a jerk! I was at a hotel. Long story. Very long story, so, tell me about yourself."

Just when I was getting ready to go into a long spiel about my life, my phone vibrated in my pocket. I pulled it out, and it was my alarm that I have set for my clients so I wouldn't forget. It lets me know when I have an hour before the start time. I cleared the alarm and put it back in my pocket. My mind instantly started spinning because I forgot this woman likes that extra freaky shit. It would seriously take an hour to get my car, and then come back to the hotel. I ain't want to lose no money, so I was going to have to improvise.

"Sorry, Prep School. I wish I could continue this conversation, but I have to go. We can pick back up where we left off soon. Is that alright with you?"

"Sure," she solemnly said.

As much as I wanted to stay, this conversation wasn't going to get me five thousand dollars.

∞

"Damn, you got the best dick I have evvverrrr had!" Tracey screamed under me as I pinned her face down in the pillow with one hand, while holding her arm behind her back with the other one.

I kept my bottom lip tucked in between my teeth while I fucked her like it was going out of style.

"Fuuckkk, Malice. You know how to fuck me like I like. Fuck! Fuck! This pussy is cumming! Please, hit it harder!"

"Squirt on this dick then," I growled as I started slamming into her hard as I could.

"Malice, pleeeasssseeee!"

I pulled out of her, and her pussy squirted out like a broken faucet. I shook my head at how I'm able to do to these women what their husbands failed to do. My other client told me that as long as she'd been fucking, she ain't never squirted, and I made her do that. She paid me an extra thousand dollars for making her do that.

"Malice, you are about to have a frequent client. Maybe once every week, or two. You are much longer and wider than my husband, so we might have to keep it at every two weeks," she said as she got herself together.

I smirked to myself because I have heard that so many times. It was so crazy that women really didn't understand the power of Kegels. Trust me, I learned so much about the human body in school, but after Cat encouraged me, I took an online Human Sexuality and Women's Health course, after I got my GED. I knew how to please *her*, but I wanted to please my other clients as well. Those classes, plus a lot of practice, I know I can make any woman cum and squirt, either from my fingers, my tongue, my dick, or all three.

"I'm going to get out of here," I said. "You know how to find me."

I left out of the room and went down to my motorcycle. My phone was vibrating in my pocket, and I pulled it out and it was Kam's work phone. I answered, and slowly put the phone next to my ear. She didn't say anything, and neither did I. This was weird.

She must have butt dialed me. She didn't mean to call me, I thought to myself. I was just getting ready to hang up when she called my name.

"Malice, are you there?" she asked.

"Yeah, I'm here. What's up, Prep School? You alright?"

"A normal person says hello when they pick up the phone," she laughed. "Um, yeah. I was just wondering if everything was okay. You had to rush out quickly earlier. No biggie," she said.

"Yeah, everything is fine, lil' woman. Thank you for checking on me. Um, we can do something again, if you want. It's completely up to you."

"Um, what you mean do something?"

"Whatever you want to do. The world is yours, I'm just living in it."

She giggled, and I smiled inadvertently.

"Do you always say that cheesy line, Mr. Malice?"

"Nah, I really don't. Feel special."

She giggled again, and I knew that she was smiling, which in turn made me smile again. There was an awkward silence like she was waiting on me to say something.

"So, Prep School, I have to get going, and I don't talk on the phone while riding my bike. I don't have the Bluetooth set up in my helmet, so I got to let you go. Can I call you later tonight or something?"

"Sure, Malice. Be safe on that death trap."

"Wow! Even if I was afraid of dying, that wouldn't make me feel any better. I think I'll do just fine. You just stay up and wait for my phone call. How about that?"

"Yes, sir. Be safe," she said and hung up the phone.

I put the phone back in my pocket and revved the engine on my motorcycle. I pulled out, and headed towards my storage unit to get my car. The storage unit was an hour away, so I had time to clear my mind. I hoped that getting this information from Kam was going to be easy because I would hate for her to catch feelings for me and then I just end the shit.

Here is the thing, I can't allow myself to fall for a woman right now because they are all scandalous. I mean, look at what I do to get money. I'll be damn if I fall in love with a woman and she be taking my hard-earned money to give to another man to get dicked down. Shit, if I was any of those women's husbands, I'd kill them and me. If I ever get in a relationship, I swear I'll take that shit serious. That's why I got to be completely off this fucking for money shit before I get in a relationship.

I pulled up to my storage, replaced my car with my motorcycle, and headed to my place of living. The place I share with my brother was cool. It was a four- bedroom and four-bathroom place. One of the extra rooms was a game and movie room, and the other room was a guest room, but no one hardly came out here to our house, since you know Mayhem is deep in the game. When I made it home, I pulled my car into the two-car garage. Mayhem was home, but I'm sure he was asleep. When I made it in the house, I stood under the hot water, showering for thirty minutes.

As soon as I was comfortable in the bed, I pulled out my phone and called Kam. She answered on the first ring.

"Hello," she answered the phone sleepily.

"You sleep, mama?" I asked.

"I was on my way, but I'm happy that you kept your word and called me." She shuffled in the background. "I never been called mama before. It's kind of sexy," she giggled.

"I'll call you whatever you want…mama."

For the rest of the night, we talked on the phone. I left out what I did for a living and only told her the good stuff. I'm sure she did the same. I prayed that I got the information I needed soon, because if my heart kept fluttering every time she giggled, this wouldn't end good.

Kambridge

When I left the restaurant yesterday, I dropped my prescription off and waited for my meds to get finished before I went and got me another room for the night. I still didn't want to be around anyone. I figured that if I got my own place, it would be so serene. The only time my parents' house is serene is when I'm sleep and my door is locked, knowing that my dad won't come in and beat my ass for no reason.

Also, yesterday was very interesting to say the least. I wasn't expecting to get fed by the second meanest man in the world. My dad is the first. I wasn't expecting to be on the phone with him for a couple of hours before he fell asleep on me. I actually stayed on the phone and listened to him breathe for like an hour. I felt like a creep. It was like a light snore, and I could tell that he was extremely tired. I learned a lot about him, and felt bad for being judgmental in the restaurant. I told him that I thought he was a drug dealer, and he laughed, telling me that I probably thought all black men I saw were drug dealers. I told him just the ones who have a million tats, carry a gun, and curse a lot. He didn't think that was funny.

He told me that he was in school for Business, and that he already has his Barber and Cosmetology license. He told me that he could whip me up a style, but I told him I wouldn't let him touch my hair with a ten-foot long pair of flat-irons. He told me about his plans to open up his own barbershop, and how he wants it to be men on one side and women on the other, basically like a whole salon, including Estheticians, massage therapists, mani and pedicurists. This shit warmed my heart because I ain't talked to a black man that didn't want to be a rapper or drug dealer. Well, I don't get to talk to that many black men, but I do have social media, and that's what it seems like they all want to be these days.

Today I was going home after being gone for three days. I had never been away from home this long. I wasn't sure what the reaction was going to be when I went home. I mean, I'm sure my dad could have found me. I pulled up to my house and everyone's cars were in the yard, including Connor's, and I honestly didn't want to see him, but I did want to know what they were arguing about a few days ago.

Grabbing my bags, I got out of the car. I took a deep breath before I walked inside the house. I could hear the chatter, and the moment I stepped inside of the dining room, the chatter ceased. Everyone stared at me like I had snakes coming out of my head. My sister jumped up and brought me in for an embrace. I winced a little from the pain her bear hug caused. I hugged her back, and my brother brought me in for an embrace as well. My mom walked up to me and hugged me, but my arms fell limp to my side. Grabbing me by the shoulders, she pushed me back a little so she could get a good look in my face. She pulled me back in for another embrace, but same as before, I kept my arms at my side. I just didn't want to hug my mom at that moment. Sometimes, I felt like she could do more to stop her husband from fucking with me the way that he does, but she doesn't.

"Kambridge, where were you? What happened to you? I was worried sick about you, baby," Connor said as he tried to hug me, but I blocked him. I truly wasn't fucking with him at that moment either.

"Kam, I would like to have a word with you in my office...now," my dad calmly said, and walked out of the dining room.

Slowly, I followed my dad to his office that was at the other end of the house. I made sure to stay at least five feet behind him. I ain't know if he would turn around and backhand me at any moment. When we made it to his office, he sat down in his chair while I stood at the door. I didn't want to be close to him. I couldn't be close to him.

"COME HERE!" he yelled.

The bass in his voice made my heart palpitate. I walked closer to him, and slowly slid into the chair in front of him.

"So, what do you have for me?" he asked getting straight to the point.

"Right to it, huh? Not, Kam, why are those bandages on your wrists? Not, Kam, I missed you, and I'm sorry for abusing you for the umpteenth time. Not, Kam... wait a minute, just my mom been combing the streets looking for me. You are acting like you didn't know where I was. Nothing slips by Judge⊠"

"Enough, Kambridge, before I come across this desk. I knew where you were staying, of course, and your mom never asked, so I didn't tell. The *only* reason I didn't come drag you out of that mothafuckin' hotel by your ugly ass, big ass hair, was because I thought you were there getting to know Malice so you could get me what the fuck I need so I can lock his father and brother away for the rest of their lives. So, back to my original question, what… do… you… have… for… me?"

He asked that last question in such a sinister way to the point where I know that he was about to jump on me if I don't give him what he wanted. My eyes teared up at the hair comment because that is the one thing that I loved about myself, and he was trying to take that away from me.

"I… I don't have anything." I swallowed the lump in my throat. "He hasn't talked about his father, or his brother in detail."

"Are you doing everything that you can do to get that information from him?" he asked through gritted teeth.

"Yes, I asked him about his father. He said that he didn't want to talk about it. What more can I do?"

Waiting for his answer, I had a feeling about what he was going to say, but I just had to hear it come out of his mouth. I had to hear what lengths my father wanted me to go to satisfy his fucking ego.

"Kam, fuck him! He'll tell you everything you need to know. Suck his dick! I'm sure you're good at it. Don't act like you so innocent. I have cameras in every room of my house."

I couldn't stop the tears from falling because every time I think my dad can't get any lower, he proves me wrong.

"You watch Connor's and my intimate moments? That's sick! That's really sick! I still have my cherry, and I'm giving it to my husband," I whispered.

"Humph, so Connor be fucking you in your ass, I guess? You

think that cracker is going to marry you? Please! He just using you until he gets that black pussy, and after a couple of times of hitting it, he's going to leave. He don't want no black girl on his arm. Trust me. All those study days he be having at his friend's house, studying for the bar as he calls it, most of them have been spent at his office, mingling amongst his colleagues, that he wouldn't dare invite you to. You better wake up, Kambridge. He will never marry you."

"You're saying all of this to say what, huh? No matter what you say, I'm not about to compromise my morals to appease you and your ego, Judge Kason. I'm not having sex with Malice. My vagina will just be another piece of vagina to him. There is no guarantee that he will tell me anything then. So, I would have lost my virginity for no reason at all," I seethed through my tears.

I excused myself to the nearest bathroom, and let out the gut wrenching cry that I was holding in. I knew that I would never get any peace in this house if I didn't get any information for him. The door crashed in and it was my dad.

Whap!

He punched me so hard in my stomach that I lost the wind in my body.

"Dry them crocodile ass tears and get your ass back in there, and you better act like this didn't happen. I want my information too, Kambridge," he said and shut the bathroom door.

I finally caught my breath and got myself together so I could go back out to the table where everyone else was. Faking a smile, I walked back in the dining room and took my seat next to Connor. He wrapped his arm around me, and all I could think about was the fact that he lied to me about his whereabouts. For the next two hours, we sat there, ate, and had meaningless conversations. My body was on autopilot, and I only spoke when I was spoken to.

∞

Laying in the bed that night, I asked Connor, "You do love me, right?"

I was sort of hoping that he would go home, so I could call Malice so he could make me laugh.

"Yeah, why would you ask me something like that, Kam? You are the light of my life. I don't know what I would do without you," he said as he slid the sleeves of my sleeping shirt down. "You know I hate to see your skin all tore up like that."

Closing my eyes for a moment, I gathered my thoughts.

"Connor, if you love me, and I am the *light of your life*, why do you lie to me?"

"What did I lie to you about?"

"Your office parties. I'm never invited. Why is that? The argument I rolled up on between you and Holly, what was that about? Connor, now is not the time to lie to me, okay? You have one time to tell me the truth, and please don't let me find out anything different. I hate for us to waste ten years, but I promise you⌧"

"Kam, look, baby, I'm sorry for lying to you, but I know you don't like my friends or colleagues, and I wouldn't want to bring you there, knowing that you would be uncomfortable. That argument with

Holly was because I didn't want to go out for drinks with them, and she thinks that you are a distraction, per usual. Look at me, Kam. I love you so much. I have given you a decade of my life, and I can't wait to marry you and give you my kids."

"You still could have asked, Connor. You didn't even extend the courtesy, which has me questioning your feelings towards me."

"You don't ever have to question my feelings for you," he said.

He pulled the covers back and climbed on top of me, and my body tensed up at the thought of a camera being in my room. I didn't want to alert Connor of it, so I just kept that new-found information to myself. He slowly slid my gown up all the way, but he didn't pull it off. He sucked on my nipples and then bit it. He knew that I hated that.

"Don't bite it, Connor," I ordered.

"Sorry, chocolate."

He kissed on the other one, and then kissed all the way down to my navel. He spread my legs and kissed on my pussy. He licked up and down my pussy, making her get wet. I tried to enjoy what he was doing to me, but my mind was on the fact that my dad could be watching me right now. My mind was on this mission that my dad wanted me to do, and the person that he wanted me to get the information from… Malice.

"KAM! Why haven't you cum yet? I've been down here ten minutes," Connor growled.

I looked down into a red-faced Connor. It's crazy to me that a person who loves to eat pussy only eats for ten minutes, and then be done, but he expected me to suck his dick until I turned blue in the face. He truly be having me fucked up.

"My mind…"

"Your mind, what? Your mind is on another nigga?"

It was like I heard a record scratch in my head.

"Connor, get out," I snapped.

I couldn't believe that he had said that shit. If it came out that easy then I'm sure he says that shit when he was with his racist ass friends.

"But--"

"But, nothing. Connor, there is no excuse for what you said. It rolled off your tongue so easily, so I know it rolls off your tongue with your friends, and you probably change the ending. Please get out. I don't want to see you for a little minute. We need a break."

"Nah, Kam. We don't need a break. I'm so sorry. Truly. I'm so sorry. Pleasee," he begged.

Before I could respond, Connor ducked his head back between my legs and started slurping on my pussy like his life depended on it. Well, in a sense, it did. I tried to make myself cum, but it was no use. My mind was too preoccupied. He kissed up my stomach, and then tried to kiss my lips, but I turned my head.

"Connor, get out!" I said. "Tell Kade to let you out. I'll call you when I'm ready to talk to you."

Before he could respond, my work phone rang. I tensed up and tried not to smile at the fact that the only reason my work phone would ring this late would be because Malice is calling.

"Why the fuck your work phone ringing this late? Who the fuck calling you?" Connor snapped.

"Connor, I'm sitting here looking in your fucking face. How the fuck would I know who is calling my phone? Why you still sitting here anyway? Get out."

"When you started doing all this cursing? You barely used to curse, but now you cursing every other word. You alright?"

I laughed to myself because Malice was already rubbing off on me, and we don't even have a formal relationship; hell, we not even friends. While I was deep in thought, Connor left out of my room and slammed the door. I looked out the window long enough to see him jump in his car and drive off. I'm sure I'd have a long text message in the morning about how much he loves me, cares for me, worships the ground that I walk on. It's never ending with him.

As I was grabbing my phone out my purse, Kade walked in and sat on my bed. He took my ankles in his hand, pulling my feet in his lap. He started massaging my feet. I laid back and enjoyed the feeling.

"Kam, I want you to know that you are so beautiful, you know that? Don't let what Dad says change that. One day you are going to find a man that loves you more than life itself, and when you do, you're going to damn near forget all those things that Dad said and did to you. I try to treat you how you need and want to be treated, but I'm just your brother, and I can only do so much," he laughed. "I wish I knew why dad was the way he was to you. Every time I try to talk to him about it, he tells me to mind my business."

"Kade, can you just get your own place and I move in with you? I don't want to live here anymore, and I'm just tired. Did I tell you what he wants me to do?"

"Nah, guh! What he wants you to do?" Kade whispered.

I laughed at the fact that Kade was talking to me like he was really my best friend. I was getting ready to speak when I thought about the cameras that were in the room. I got up and put on my slippers. I pulled Kade out the room, and told him that we have to go outside. He put the code in, and we walked outside. Kade was too quick for me to remember it though.

"Why you got me out here, lil' woman?"

"So, I brought you out here because dad has cameras in the house. He informed me that he saw me and Connor doing *things*. All that came about because he told me that I need to do *whatever I have to do* to get information from Malice to lock up his brother and his father. I told him that I wasn't losing my virginity to him because, honestly, I'm sure my vagina is just another vagina to him."

My brother sat there with an amused look on his face, and it kind of threw me off.

"You can't do that," he exclaimed.

"I know I can't do that. I don't want to do that. Malice may kill me, and then he told me that I would have to testify against them in court. I mean, just because those two are arrested doesn't mean that there are other people that may not come after me. He can't protect me from hundreds of people. I know how gangs work. I watched *Cocaine Cowboys* with that Charles dude, and Griselda Blanco. She was putting hits out on that dude from behind bars."

"Wait, let's back up. How do you know Malice?"

"Um, he came into my store and got some shirts. He's just been a pain in my ass ever since. He knows about Malice because he dropped me off at home after I snuck out to Mayhem's party, and Shelly went to do whatever she was doing. How do you know Malice?"

"I work for his brother," he whispered.

"KADE!" I screamed.

I did not want my brother to become one of those dudes that runs the streets. He has a degree in Business for Christ's sake.

"Stop. I don't deal drugs or nothing like that. I'm his accountant. I move his money around and make sure everyone is getting what they are supposed to be getting, that's all. I don't touch the drugs or none of that shit. I promise." He raised his hands in the air. "I only smoke a little weed every now and then. That is why I'm never home. His money never ever stops, so I'm always on the move."

"Wow! All this time, I thought you were just sleeping around with lots of women and never came home," I chuckled.

"Yeah, the women come with working for him. When you are associated with the Baileys, the women flock to you regardless. Once you are seen with them, women automatically think you are somebody. Before you ask, Dad doesn't know who my client is. I'm sure if he did, he would have been asked me to set them up. He's so focused on you, and we have to keep it that way. Aight! I'm going to try and get me a place to live, and then you can move with me, and Kalena too, because if you leave, he will probably start beating on Kalena."

"More than likely he won't. He don't treat y'all the same way he treats me."

Kade and I were close, but it seems like this new piece of information made us even closer. He pulled me in for a hug and kissed me on my jaw.

"Family reunion?" we heard from the porch.

We both kind of jumped at the sound of his voice. We turned to look at our dad standing on the porch with his arms folded across his chest.

"Nah, Pops. We were just out here talking. Nothing serious. Just catching up on her time away."

"You couldn't have caught up in the house? Why you guys come out here to talk?" My dad fired off question after question.

"Dad, just chill. We needed some air," Kade said.

"Well come inside before you both catch a cold," he urged.

"Everything is going to be alright," he whispered in my ear, as he walked behind me into the house.

Kade walked me in my room, laid me down, and tucked me in. He kissed me on my forehead and reassured me again that everything was going to be okay. He walked out the room and shut the door behind him. I was too tired to check my phone to call Malice back, so I went to sleep.

Kade Lewis

After tucking Kam in, I went back to my room and turned the TV on. Shit, me and my dad tight as hell, and I didn't even know that he had cameras in the house. I'm glad that I ain't ever bring home none of my work regarding Mayhem. My heart was so heavy for the turmoil that he puts Kam through, for God only knows what reason. I asked Mom why she don't do shit about it and she just shrugs it off, but I know she knows the reason why. Hell, I even asked him why, and he told me to mind my fucking business.

Kam is my little sister, but she is also sort of kind of my best friend. She talks to me about everything, and I try to listen like a best friend instead of her brother. She even told me about the first time she had sexual relations, and that made me want to vomit, but other than that, I listen to everything. I try to treat her how our dad should be treating her, so she will know how she is supposed to be treated by a man. I treat Kalena the same way. I hate that I'm not here to defend her as much as I used to be. When she was younger and I used to come home at a decent hour, I could stop him.

Honestly, I've been wanting to move out, but my dad told me no. I tried to move out on my own, and no one would take my application because my dad had blocked me. So, I honestly had no choice but to stay. He just said it's for my protection that I stay with him. He swears some people may try to retaliate against him for locking up criminals. I told him that criminals belong in jail so people shouldn't want to retaliate against him, but that fell on deaf ears.

It's crazy how working for Mayhem could fly under the radar with him. He knows that I rent an office downtown in a lawyer's building, but he doesn't know that I only have ONE client. Mayhem pays me so damn good, and keeps me so damn busy to the point where I couldn't even take on another client if I wanted to. Mayhem knows about my father, and he told me that if any information regarding his business got back to my father or anyone that works with him, he wouldn't hesitate to kill me and anyone associated with me. Just when I was getting ready to go to sleep, my dad rushed into my room.

"Son, what was Kam talking to you about?" my dad asked.

"Nothing. The usual, rather. Telling me the reason that she left a few days ago," I lied.

"Kade, you know I'm a judge, right?"

He always said that when he knows that one of us is lying to him. You can barely get any type of lie by this man.

"Dad, she wants to move out, and so do I. We are both grown and make our own money. We can very well take care of ourselves. No one is going to retaliate against you and harm us."

"The answer is no, and that's final. This house has more than enough space for everybody to never see each other. You bring your chicks here from time to time, and that white boy damn near lives here. So what's the problem? What are you going to do at your own house that you can't do here? Absolutely nothing. So, again, my final answer is no, so please don't bother me about it again," he snapped.

"One last question. Why don't you like Kambridge? Don't say that you do because you wouldn't beat on her the way you do if you did. Kambridge is a beautiful, chocolate, very intelligent girl, who has accomplished more than the average twenty-two-year-old. You beat her down so bad to the point where she doesn't even believe that she is beautiful anymore. Even after the way you beat her, the few times she has been to the hospital, she has never ratted you out when she could have."

He stared at me for a minute, brushed his hand down his wavy hair, and blew out a sigh of frustration. One would have thought that he was about to give me some heavy ass information.

"This is grown man business. Mind your business, Kade," he snapped and walked out of the room.

I should have known that he wasn't going to say shit about that. Honestly, my main focus was trying to keep Kam safe in all this bullshit because I have seen first-hand what can happen to people who cross the Baileys. I ain't even touching the drugs, but that nigga drove me to an underground warehouse where he killed people, and told me that's where I would end up. I would never cross him, and I wouldn't let my sister cross that nigga either.

As a big brother, I'm going to check that nigga Malice too, because if he thinks he about to fuck my sister and dump her, then it's going to be a problem as well.

∞

Walking into my office, the women were speaking to me and trying to flirt with me. I date, but not too much because how can a twenty-seven-year-old man tell a woman that he can't move out of his dad's house because his father is fearful? Besides, I haven't even dated a woman that I like enough to even explain my situation to them, so whatever. My desk was full of paperwork from Mayhem's businesses. I worked for a few hours before I left my office for lunch. I went to a restaurant where Mayhem and his brother frequented from time to time. I needed to holler at Malice. As soon as I walked in, I told the receptionist who I was there to see, and she told me that they had just been seated.

Walking over to the table, my heart was beating fast because I know what both niggas were capable of, but my sister's heart and life is on the line.

"What's up, Kade? Everything good?" Mayhem stood and dapped me up.

Malice was staring at his phone, but gave me a head nod. Mayhem sat back down, and I turned my attention back to Malice.

"Malice, I just wanted to let you know that Kambridge is my sister, and if you fuck her over, I won't hesitate to beat your ass. I know what you capable of, but I'm capable of some shit too, my nigga!" I spoke.

Malice let out a smooth chuckle like he didn't give a fuck what I was saying. He slid out the booth and got eye level with me. He cocked his head to the side and smiled at me. He bit the bottom of his lip and continued to give me a glare.

"You're not intimidating me, homeboy!" I seethed.

"I'm not trying to intimidate you, Kade. I'm actually proud of you for stepping to me like a real nigga for your sister. If I had a sister I would do the same thing, but what I will tell you is that Kam is grown, and whatever she wants to do, we will do," he calmly said.

"Look, Malice. I don't know what type of bitches you into, but my sister not like that. She is beautiful, she is kind, smart, owns her own fucking business, and makes her own money. She don't need you for any of that shit. If you only trying to get some pussy from her, then you need to move the fuck around--"

"Boy, do you know who you talking to?" Mayhem cut me off, but I ignored him.

"--because LIKE I SAID before, Kam ain't on no hoe shit. She don't need you for your money, your clout, or nothing, fam. Only step to my sister if you trying to show her how a woman should be treated; anything other than that, leave her alone. I'll kill and die behind mine," I snapped.

He looked at Mayhem and chuckled. "Mayhem, this prep school ass nigga got some heart. Who would have thought that shit?" He laughed and then focused back on me. "Yours," he whispered. "*You'll die behind yours*," he mocked me. "How you'll kill behind yours when y'all bitch ass daddy is still--"

WHAP!

I knew what he was going to say and I punched Malice in his face with all my might. My lick dazed him for only a few seconds, before we were in an all-out brawl in the damn restaurant. We were both landing licks on each other. Somehow, Malice got me in a chokehold and was squeezing the life out of me. I knew that nigga was about to end me. Just when my last breath was about to make me pass out, Mayhem saved my life.

"ENOUGH!!" Mayhem stood and yelled.

Malice dropped me on command, and I fell to the floor trying to catch my breath. Mayhem stood and helped me up. I dusted myself off and glared at Malice who was now sitting in the position he was in when I first walked in.

"Kade, The only reason why I'm not hitting you with some hot lead right now is because I got MAD respect for a nigga that can walk up to a Bailey and then hit him. If I had a sister, I would have done the same thing, my nigga. You got that shit off your chest. Dap Malice up, and this shit is over with. Next time you run up on him, you might not be so lucky, aight?"

I nodded my head and dapped Malice up. Surprisingly, he dapped me back up.

"Look, Malice. No hard feelings, but I really love my sister, man. If you know about that shit with my father, then y'all been talking a lot, but please, man, don't lead her on. That's all I ask. She got enough shit to deal with," I pleaded.

I hated myself because my eyes watered in front of these niggas, but my sister was a sensitive subject for me. I walked away from them and headed to my car. The fresh air hit my face making my eyes dry up. I was hoping that he would leave her alone so she won't get wrapped up in my dad's shit with Korupt. I don't know what them two got going on, but whatever it is, my dad needed to leave my sister out of it.

Malice

*O*wweee, my fucking jaw was stinging like a mothafucka, and I knew that the shit was going to be bruised tomorrow. But, I could honestly say that I wasn't pissed about Kade stepping to me like a boss about his sister. That showed me that the nigga was not afraid to die behind his sister. Honestly, I was just baiting him about their dad shit. She never told me who gave her the bruises, but Kade gave me the confirmation that I wanted. Now I was pissed that she's even in the house with that nigga. I was going to try and hold off as long as I could without mentioning it, but if Kam and her brother are close like he says they are, he is probably going to tell her about the fight that took place in here.

I kept looking down at my phone because I didn't want to meet Mayhem's glare. I was looking at my phone because I was wondering why Kam hadn't text me, nor called me back, since I low-key blew her phone up last night. I wanted to apologize for going to sleep on her the previous night we talked on the phone, but a nigga was tired. I looked at the time on the phone, and it said three hours, which meant that she was listening to a nigga sleep on the phone. She was kind of funny in her own little way, too. She always had some type of joke for something.

"You can keep on ignoring me if you want to, but guess who ain't leaving this seat until I get some answers. You got your ass whooped by a nigga that wore a blazer with a patch on it to school. Nigga, what the fuck?"

I clearly could have killed that nigga, but because he got more than two licks off me, and hit me first, I lost the fight. According to Mayhem, winning a fight is knocking a nigga out in two licks or less."

"Mayhem, she told me she had a brother, but she ain't told me no names. That's it, fam. The girl that did my jerseys, that's his sister. She got her own store on the other side. She real cool."

"Leave her alone, Malice. She's young, and apparently got a lot going on. Her brother is the best damn accountant I ever had. I don't need him stressed. One bad day for him, and my money is lost. You are not capable of giving that girl what she desires, especially with…you know what you do to get dough. You get where I'm going with this, fam?"

"I'm hearing you, fam, but we just friends. Two people that just keep crossing each other's path. I walked in her shop, then I saw her in the movies, and then back at her shop. I saw her at your party, and she looked completely out of place. You can tell her dad sheltered her a lot. She looked terrified to be in there. You know Shelly, her friend. She told me that the other night when we were on the phone."

"Wait, lil' white honey that keep trying to get with me, is the girl you just described to me, friend? How that happen?"

"Man, she said that she is the only girl that made her feel really comfortable at her school."

"I guess, but you need you leave that girl alone. Seriously."

"Listen, I know you and Dad cool, so did he tell you about the thing that he wanted me to do? He wants me to use Kam. He said that her dad stole some gold from him, and if I get the gold then he will give me five hundred racks out of the two million. You know what I could do what five hundred racks, big bro?"

"Phoenix… look at me. Stay away from that girl and that mess with her dad, and OUR dad. I been told dad to leave that gold shit alone. He ain't even missing that two million. If he wants that shit then he need to settle that shit like a grown man, and not use his son to get in the head of a young girl. Stay away from that, Phoenix. How you know that trick ain't trying to use you the same way you trying to use her, huh?"

I knew my brother was dead ass serious because that is the only time he called me by my real name. I never thought about that shit either. She don't seem like she would try to use a nigga that way. She ain't even ask me about none of my family. I volunteered the information, but I ain't tell her nothing that everybody don't already know.

"See, I can tell the way your eyebrows are furrowing together that you didn't even think about that shit. I'mma tell you again to stay away from that girl. Now, look, I know that you grown and you probably going to talk to her anyway. If you do, keep that girl out our family business. Do I make myself clear?"

I nodded my head. My brother was right. I would probably still talk to her, though. We are really just friends. Honestly, I can read right through Kambridge to be honest. She wears every emotion on her face, and I do mean every one of them. My brother and I finished eating in silence. We left the restaurant and he told me that he would see me at the house. I only had one class earlier today, so I headed to the apartment to cut a few people's heads who were waiting on me. I'm relieved that I ain't have to fuck today. That means I get to go home and fucking chill for a change. Catch up on some reading or something.

I told one person to meet me at the apartment, and when I pulled up, it was like eight people waiting. I'm grateful for being able to build my clientele, but I was for sure thinking that I was going to get home and could chill for the rest of the day. I got out and unlocked the door. Everybody made themselves comfortable. I'm normally talkative, but everything Mayhem said to me was on my mind. So I just listened to the dudes give each other advice on different shit. Three hours later, I was cleaning up my shop and getting ready to get out of here. A part of me knew I should have went straight home, but another part of me wanted to see that black ass girl, and guess what? I was on my way across town to see her.

It took me an hour with traffic to get across town, and I made it right at fifteen minutes after seven. The store was dark, but it wasn't pitch black. I could see the light from the back room. Her car was still out front so I knew she was in there. I slightly pulled on the door handle and it opened right up. Her keys were in the door. I shook my head at how careless she was for leaving her keys in the door. I locked the door and took the keys out of the hole. I rang the bell twice and there was nothing. So, I unhooked the latch and let myself behind the counter. I peeked in the back, and I could see her with her noise cancellation Beats by Dre covering her ears.

"Seems like your readdddddyyyyy," she sang along with R. Kelly in her ears while swaying her barely there hips. She has the rhythm of a newborn deer trying to walk. "Boy are you rrreeeaaadddyyyy." She continued to sing as she slammed the machine down on some shirts.

She couldn't even hear me, nor see me, but I was chuckling as she continued to sing and dance. We both have very similar taste in music. She had on a long sleeve t-shirt dress like she always wears. It stopped right in the middle of her thighs. Not being able to take it much longer, I crept up behind her, latched onto her waist and started swaying along with her. She snatched her headphones off and turned around and let out a gasp.

"Malice, what the heck are you doing breaking in here like that, and what happened to your face!"

I could see her heart beating through that dress she was wearing. I held the keys up and dropped them in her hand.

"You left the door unlocked. I suppose you meant to lock it. You need to stop being so fucking careless, ma. I could have been anybody walking up in this bitch. You could have been raped and murdered by now. I've been standing there for the last ten minutes watching you look like an elephant trying to stand up for the first time. You ain't got no cameras up in this bitch?"

"You're a creep for watching me like that," she said, rolling her eyes.

"You listen to people breathe on the phone, so who really is the creep here?"

She squinted her eyes at me before replying, "I have cameras in

115

here. I thought the door was locked so I didn't look at the cameras. Sorry, father, I will make sure the door is locked next time."

"Don't call me your father, ever! No fucking comparison."

She rolled her eyes again and then touched the bruise on my face. She started randomly laughing.

"Did the school bully take little Malice's lunch money, and then sock him in his little red face?" she said as if she was talking to a baby.

I moved my face out of her hand because I ain't see shit funny. She turned to take the shirts off the machine.

"What happened to your face though? Are you okay?"

"You first. Tell me about your bruises and I'll tell you about mine," I countered.

"That's not fair, Malice!" She stomped her foot and crossed her arms across her chest like a child.

"Life's not fair, Kambridge," I countered and cocked my head to the side.

She turned around to me with tears in her eyes, and said, "Do I have to tell you?"

"Your tears not fucking with me, Kambridge," I lied. They were fucking with me tough because I already knew, but I wanted to hear it from her mouth.

"Alright. Give me a second, and we can go somewhere to talk. Okay?"

She turned around and started finishing the shirts she was working on.

"Can I help you?"

She looked at me with a shocked look on her face. She told me to make sure the shirts were straight with no wrinkles on the machine. She placed the logo on the shirt and then placed my hand on the bar. She put her hand on top of mine and we slowly brought the top down.

"You have to bring the top down slow because if you bring it down to fast, the wind from the machine will move the logo and have it crooked on the shirt. Then you have to start all the way over or listen to a screeching like voice in your ear about their shirt," she laughed. "*You fucked my shirt up, you black bitch,*" she said in a high pitch voice, sounding just like those bitches in the hood. I couldn't help but chuckle.

We waited for a second, and she put her hand back on mine and lifted it up.

"Now, grab that sheet by both ends and pull it up slowly," she instructed.

I did what she said, and it was like magic. It was perfect.

"Look at you. I may have to hire you to help me do this on the days I'm backed up," she chuckled.

For the next hour, she did like twenty shirts, and I did like three, but it was cool. I was so focused on trying not to fuck up these shirts that I couldn't even talk, and she didn't mind it. She folded the shirts and placed them in the box. I helped her clean the machines and the back room. After we were done cleaning, I made sure she locked the door, and I walked her to her car.

"Malice, you really have a sexy ass car. Damn! I'm getting me one of those in three years, and I'm going to pay for it cash money."

"Alright, I'll let you drive mine, and I'll drive yours. Follow me though. Don't fuck my shit up. It has a chip in it, which makes it go dumb fast. You know you can't drive. You still owe me for fucking up my car," I laughed.

"Malice, it was barely a scratch on it. Chill. I gave you my insurance information."

I walked her over to my car and made sure she was comfortable, before I jumped in her car. I prayed that I didn't regret this decision, but I was taking her to the house I shared with my brother. I knew that he was going to be pissed, but I would handle him accordingly. I'm a family first type of nigga, and if Kam does anything to jeopardize my family, I'll kill her. I've never killed before, but I wouldn't hesitate.

Kambridge

I could not contain my excitement as I slid in the seats of Malice's Mercedes. I know I rode in here when he brought me home a couple of weeks ago, but it doesn't compare to sitting on the driver's side. His words faded out as I started touching all the buttons in the car, adjusting the seat, and finding a good radio station.

"KAMBRIDGE!" he yelled my name, making me jump.

"Yes… yes, I heard you. You don't have to scream, sheesh."

"Well, what did I say?"

I held a tight grip on the steering wheel, and I looked at him with my lips folded in my mouth. He knew that I didn't hear a word he said. I was just excited to be sitting in the seat of my dream car.

"Um, um, you said, ummm☒"

"Don't touch the red but☒"

"The red button, right…right."

"Kam, I'm serious. Don't under no circumstances touch it. You can't even accidentally touch it because it's up there," he said pointing to the top of the radio.

"What does it do? If I might ask," I said, glaring at it like a kid in a candy store.

The red button was glowing, and it was making me get antsy. You know how back when you were younger when your mom told you not to touch the stove because it was hot, and you didn't listen and had to find out for yourself? This is what I feel like right now, staring at this button.

"Don't worry about what it do! I'll let you push it another day," he said.

I smiled at him and watched him walk over to my car. The way he walked had me squeezing my legs together tightly. He walked with confidence and his head held high. His Levi jeans that sat at his waist turned me on even more, and I wasn't supposed to be getting turned on by him. He kept the door open while he was adjusting the seat. I was staring at him, but he wouldn't know because his tint was dark as fuck, and more than likely illegal.

He closed the door, and sped off in my car. I put my foot on the gas just a tiny bit, and damn near burnt rubber out of the parking lot. This car will go fast, and I love it. We rode for like thirty minutes before we turned into a nice ass neighborhood, not even far from my neighborhood. He pulled in the yard, let the garage door up, and I'm assuming he wanted me to pull his car in, so that's what I did.

"Whose house is this?" I whispered, walking up to him.

"Why are you whispering?" he whispered back.

"I don't know. I ain't know if your parents would be home or something. You might get in trouble," I said.

"You serious? This my house. Me and my brother's house," he said in a snappy tone.

I didn't respond while I followed him up the stairs to the front door. This house was amazing. We walked in the house, and the lights automatically came on.

"Take them lil' ugly shoes off before you scratch up my hardwood floors, and I have to tap that lil' ass," he said.

I picked up my shoes and carried them. We left out that room, and the lights went off, and then the lights in the hallway came on.

"This house is like a smart house. Is this whole house motion activated?" I asked out of curiosity.

"Yeah, it is. Saves money."

I followed him as he gave me a tour of the house. I was so impressed with the way the lights were set up in his house. He took me on the roof, and there was an in-ground pool. A regular sized pool on the roof. I mean two of his houses could fit in mine, but his house way cooler.

"Who the hell puts a pool on a roof?" I asked him as we walked back inside.

"Eh, I ain't build this house. I don't know, but I reckon since there was no room in the back, there was only one place left to put it."

"Shut up."

We went in his room, and the lights came on. He sat on his bed, and I sat in the chair next to his bed. His room was about the same size as mine and set up like a bachelor pad, like Kade's room. Big ass flat screen on the wall with game consoles, and the room was very clean. He had a big ass mirror on the wall. I guess he got to look at himself before he left the house.

"Your girlfriend knows I'm here?" I asked, breaking the silence in the room.

"I'm single, what about you?"

"Same here," I lied.

That shit rolled right off my tongue like it was nothing. My dad told me to do whatever I had to do, and if I had to lie then that's what I had to do. I'd been ignoring Connor ever since I sent him home. He'd been apologizing and shit, but I wasn't trying to hear his ass right now.

"So, talk. Tell me about your bruises, and I will tell you about mine. Oh, don't look at me with those big ass bright eyes. I ain't forget. No one here but us. Come sit next to me and talk to me."

I moved slowly to the bed and sat down. I stared into his eyes, and his gaze was very intense. Almost intimidating.

Kambridge, do whatever you have to do! Do...whatever...you...have...to...do. I heard my dad's voice in the back of my head. We not supposed to be getting personal like this.

"Kam, baby doll. You blanking out on me. Talk to me," he whispered, sliding his hands in mine.

His hands were so smooth. You could tell this nigga didn't work outside, or never had.

"Um, my dad hates me. Well, he's hot and cold with me. Some days he acts like the best dad in the world, and some days he acts like I'm some bitch off the street who stole from him. He beats me. Malice, you would think after the first couple of times he put me in the hospital that he would stop. He told me that he was the police, and that he could get away with killing me. I don't even understand what I did wrong. My mom doesn't stop him. My baby sister cries, and my brother is hardly home to stop him anymore. So, he just stops when I pass the fuck out from the pain. The reason I was in the hospital was because he beat me after you dropped me off. I left and went to a hotel. They got infected, and that's where the bandages and stuff came from. She drained them and gave me a pain shot. That's it."

He stared at me for a moment before he replied, "Your brother hit me."

"My brother, Kade Lewis, hit you?" I chuckled. "Wait… why did Kade hit you? What did you say to him? My brother is not violent."

"Over you he is, apparently. What did you say to him?"

"Nothing. He asked why dad beat me the last time, and I told him it was because you dropped me off at home. I apologize for him hitting you."

"He did what any real man would do. I applaud him, but if he does that shit again, I might have to murk him."

"I'll murk you back," I replied to him while rolling my neck.

He chuckled. I got up and walked over to his wall. He had his achievements up there. I know he told me about them, but to actually see them was a different thing. He was a licensed barber, cosmetologist, and had his Associates in Business, working on his Bachelor's degree. This is fucking incredible, and I swear I hate I judged him from the beginning.

"You found a building yet for when you open up your shop?" I asked.

"Yeah, I've been looking at different places. I want the spot to be perfect, and I want to actually buy the building instead of rent because I don't want them mothafuckas to try and kick me out because a lot of niggas may be in and out of the shop. You feel me? You know how it goes. Did you buy your building, or you're renting?"

"I'm actually renting, since I opened up on my own without my dad's help. I wish I could have bought it myself. I was just trying to show him that I could be responsible, but that nigga still wouldn't let me move out. Talkin' about people may use us to retaliate against him. It's crazy."

"Damn, if a nigga gotta retaliate, your pops must be a fraud ass nigga," he said.

I turned around and shot him a look. He shrugged his shoulders. I stood in front of his mirror and looked at myself. *I'm really a beast at makeup*, I thought to myself.

"You know, Malice. Once you open your shop, we can become business partners. I'll buy a booth from you and do makeup. Work a few hours in the morning and at night. I mean, especially on the weekends. You know y'all be partying over there all the time. It may be good business for your shop. What you think?"

"Can I see you without makeup?" he asked, completely disregarding my question.

"Um, you will never see me without makeup. I'm sorry, but⬛"

"But what? You scared of what I may think about you, Kambridge? You scared that I'm not going to see you for the beautiful woman that you are? You don't need that shit on your face anyway, especially if you have a problem with your skin. You are only fixing the problem externally, not internally. What is going on with your skin that you are hiding?"

My body was frozen in place because how the hell we get from becoming business partners to him trying to see me without my makeup? These acne scars were going to be the death of me. I was trying not to tear up, but this insecurity of mine was so heavy, and it was just easier to cover it up and not talk about versus deal with it head on.

In the mirror, I could see him scooting the chair in front of him. He walked in the bathroom. He stayed in there for a minute, but I could hear the water running. He came out with a small tub, a towel, and a bottle of something.

"Come sit," he ordered.

"You're not seeing me without makeup. Not yet," I said.

"Come sit," he said again.

"Did you hear what I said?" I asked with an attitude.

"Did you hear what I...said. Come sit, now!" he said with much more force.

It felt like I had cement blocks tied to my legs trying to walk over to the seat. I kept trying to blink my eyes really quickly so I wouldn't cry in front him. I plopped down in the seat with an attitude.

"Who let you get away with all this attitude? Who puts up with it? Must been those white dudes at that prep school you went to, because if you were mine, your ass would be right in line. All that mouth you got would have been straight nipped in the bud, sweetheart."

I didn't reply to him, but he was right. When I'm talking crazy to Connor, he lets me get away with that shit. He'd be trying to console me while I'm going off on him. Depending on the situation, it's mostly my way or no way.

He pressed the soap out of the bottle, rubbed his hands together, and started rubbing his hands in a circular motion on my face.

"Don't worry, it's just Cetaphil mixed with some oils that keep your skin moisturized long after you washed your face off."

His hands felt so good on my face, but I was starting to feel naked. He was making me vulnerable, and I hated it. The more I felt the makeup come off my face, the more my eyes welled up with tears. I knew the minute I opened my eyes, the tears were going to fall. He massaged my face for a couple more minutes, and then picked up the towel out of the small tub, and wiped my face so slow. Biting the inside of my cheek used to stop me from crying, but sitting here in front of him, the tears were falling still. I hate him. I hate this man. My heart was beating so fast because I knew he thought I was such an ugly duckling now and was going to kick me out of his house.

"Now, look at you! Come here." He pulled me out the seat and into the mirror. "You see how much better you look without that bozo shit on your face? Let your face breathe, Kam. The more you pile that shit on there, the more you fuck it up. Why you crying, man?"

I humped my shoulders up and down, but I knew why I was crying.

"Can I see all of your scars? I wanna see all of you, Kambridge. I'm sick of you wearing these long sleeve shirt dresses or whatever y'all females call 'em."

"We've done enough for tonight, and plus, I'm not taking my clothes off for you. You may try to have sex with me, and nah."

"I'm trying to help you stop being insecure," he said, and tugged at the bottom of my dress. He started pulling my dress up slowly, and at the first scar I saw, I instantly started panicking. I started crying like a newborn baby. No one has seen me butt naked like this in a long time, and especially since my dad has added more bruises to my body. The first time Connor saw me naked, he told me that I needed to cover up. He hasn't seen me fully naked in years.

I raised my arms up, and let him pull the dress all the way off. I covered my small breasts with one arm and placed the other arm between my legs, in front of my bald kitty, while I continued to cry. I was naked because I didn't need to wear a bra, and I hated wearing panties. Through cloudy and teary eyes, I stared at Malice. His expression was very stern, but hadn't changed at all.

"Kambridge, you are very beautiful. How can you expect anyone else to think you beautiful, if you don't think you beautiful? You have a great business mind, but you don't have the confidence that I know is buried down in there somewhere. These scars do not define you. The right man will love you past all these scars. The right man will never tell you to cover these scars up. A nigga that don't want you to show your scars is gay, to be honest."

I chuckled at his last statement. Placing both of his index fingers on my temples, he started massaging.

"Self-love starts here. Confidence starts here. All those places you traveled, you can't tell me you ain't seen a heavy-set woman on the beach in a two piece, while you got this beautiful body covered up because of some scars. Girl, please. You better flaunt this shit," he said, and smacked me on the ass.

He went and sat on the bed and left me standing in the mirror. I picked my clothes up, but he stopped me.

"Nah, don't put them on. I like seeing you naked. It's refreshing."

"What that mean?"

"Nothing, just come over here."

I slowly sat on the bed. The room was quiet, and suddenly, Malice started rubbing my back. After his pep talk in the mirror, I started to relax.

"My name is Phoenix. Phoenix Bailey. I thought that I could at least tell you something personal about me," he said.

"How you get Malice on your credit cards if that's only your nickname?"

"That's the name I put down, and that's the name they put on there. Phoenix is such a girl name to me, honestly. My brother, Mayhem's, real name is Pryor, and my dad is Paxton, or Korupt."

"Why do y'all want evil ass aliases like that? Why the hell would you want to be called a damn Korupt? I think Paxton, Pryor, and Phoenix are decent names. I would consider naming a son of mine Phoenix or Paxton," I said.

"Oh really? Are you a virgin?" he asked.

This nigga is the king of changing the conversation right in the middle of it.

"Um, I don't know," I shrugged.

"What the hell you mean you don't know? How you don't know if you got your fucking cherry or not?"

"I don't know if I would consider myself a virgin because I have had sex before...it was anal." I whispered the last part, hoping he wouldn't hear me, and would just change the subject like he been doing.

"What was that last part? You said anal? Kam, you are having anal sex, but not vaginal sex. What's the difference, sex is sex?"

"I kinda want to save my cherry for my husband, and I like anal sex. It makes me wet. I have sucked dick and had my pussy ate before. Am I still a virgin or no?"

"I mean, virgin can mean pure or still have your che...Kambridge, you really like anal sex?" he asked me again like he just couldn't believe it.

"YESSSS! PHOENIX. Stop freaking asking me that. You creeping me out. You acting like you ain't never put your *thang* in a girl's butt before."

"I mean, I have. I just ain't... You just don't look like the type. Was he a white boy?"

I rolled my eyes at him and nodded my head.

"Aw hell, you ain't really been fucked in your ass then. I know that white dude not packing like no nigga, so you still a virgin all the way around," he laughed.

He was kind of right. Connor wasn't small, but he wasn't big either. He wasn't as thick either, but he got the job done.

"Can I make you squirt right quick?" he asked out the blue.

"Huh? How are you going to do that? You not sticking your *thang* in me."

"I ain't got to stick my *thang* in you to make you squirt. My fingers will get that done. I got a wager. If I can make you squirt, then you have to wear tank tops and no makeup for two weeks, and if I can't, then I won't curse for two weeks. Deal?"

"That ain't fair. Ugh, but whatever, deal. What do I do?"

"Relax. That's all you have to do."

He reached under the bed and pulled out a case, and put it on the bed. He opened it, but I couldn't see what he was getting. He got two boxes and put them on the bed. Reading the boxes, it was a butt plug and some lubricant.

"Um, you not sticking that in me. Ain't no telling how many... wait, why do you have that? You like⊠"

"Girl, you out your fucking mind? Don't nothing go up my ass. I like to please women, and this shit brand new. You see the plastic still on this shit," he snapped.

"Well, you know Amber Rose said Kanye likes to get⊠"

"I don't give a fuck what that peanut head bitch talking about. This is an exit only."

He had me laughing, and he looked at me like I was crazy. He sat in the chair, and while he was opening the boxes, he kept an intense glare on me. I kept looking down at my naked thighs to avoid his glare.

"Come here," he whispered.

I looked at him, and his eyes were halfway open. He looked like he was high, but he ain't smoked a thing. I guess I took too long because he gripped my thighs and slid me on his lap. My back was on the bed. I covered my face because this man had me gapped open like I was on a gynecologist table. It was a good thing that I had shaved.

"You have a pretty pussy, you know that?" he whispered, and rubbed his hand down the length of my pussy.

I shuddered at his touch. My heart rate started rising. This sexy ass man was going to send me into cardiac arrest. He opened the lubricant and lathered the butt plug in it. Placing the butt plug at the opening of my ass, I immediately started to tense up. That thing was wider than Connor, and I wasn't sure if I would be able to take it.

"Stop, don't do that. You'll like it. Relax, mama."

There goes that word. It turned me on in more ways than I could imagine. It's not so much the word itself, I guess it's the way that he said it. He started easing it inside of me, and I could feel myself getting wetter and wetter. Once it was all the way inside of me, it started vibrating.

"Whhhatttt thhhhee helllll, Phoenniixxxx?"

My body was vibrating just as fast as the butt plug was. His jaw bones flexing let me know that he was getting off on me not being able to control myself. He placed his middle and ring finger in my mouth. I started sucking on them like it was a popsicle. After I got them juicy, he slowly slid one finger inside of me and started moving it around like he was searching for something.

"Damn, you are a virgin for real. This shit snug back up in here," he whispered. "You ready for this other finger? You have to let me know when to stop. At any moment, tell me if I'm hurting you."

I couldn't reply because this butt plug was fucking my mind up.

"Kambridge, I need you to tell me if you comprehend this or not. If I'm hurting you, tell me to stop."

I nodded my head really fast. He pushed his other finger inside of me, and I threw my head back from pleasure. Pleasure that I have never felt before in my life. This man had me open and very vulnerable to him. The more he played around inside of my pussy, the more I felt myself come alive. My body started shaking faster than the damn butt plug. Phoenix was no longer pushing his fingers in and out of me. His fingers were just laying inside of me, but he was pushing upward, touching my g-spot, and I felt myself getting ready to cum.

"Malllice, fuck. I'm cumming. Oh my Godddd! Pleasee," I moaned as I released all over his fingers.

"Gooood girrrlll, but that ain't what I want, Kam. Give daddy what he wants," he whispered huskily.

He was making me lose control. I started playing with my clit, but he swatted my hand away, letting me know that he had this. I started feeling myself, and started going up down on his fingers.

"Ah shit! Come on, fuck these fingers. Gimme me what the fuck I want, Kam. Chocolate ass girl! Beautiful black ass girl! I bet you taste just like chocolate. Gimme...what...I...want..."

The sound of his voice was making me feel things I never felt before. Lust. Love. Love. No love. Can't be love! Not this soon. The pressure. The pressure on my g-spot… I can't take it.

"Ahh shit, feel like mama finna give me what I want. Let it go for me, Kam. I'm catching it all," he smirked. He quickly raised his shirt up and held it in place with his chin. "Give it to me, baby! I feel you!"

"Malliiiccceeee, ahhh, ooweee!" I screamed out in pleasure, as my juices squirted out on his abs.

"That's what I like," he laughed and turned the butt plug off. "Here, taste this," he said and stuck his middle finger in my mouth. I tightened my jaws up around it and he slowly slid it out of my mouth. He stuck his ring finger in his mouth and tasted my juices. He slowly slid the butt plug out of my ass, and put it on top of the box that he had slid from under the bed. I felt like I had run two laps fucking around with Phoenix's ass.

"Yo, Kam, you really have a pretty ass pussy, man. I mean, vagina. Pussy not a curse word though. Is it? I know this wasn't part of the deal, but you told me I curse too much anyway. So, if you can't wear makeup or cover up for two weeks, then I won't curse."

I laughed. "Anything you wouldn't say around your grandma is a curse word. You figure it out."

Before he could say anything else, his phone went off, and it was that stupid ass alarm that went off when we were out to eat. He looked at his phone, made a face, and then put it in his pocket.

"Everything okay?" I asked.

"Yeah. I'm about to jump in the shower. You want to stay here while I shower, or do you want to leave? I'm cool with either choice."

The clock on his nightstand read 10:30, so it was time for me to be making it home anyway before the big bad wolf strikes.

"Nah, I have to go anyway. I'll call you when I get in bed."

I put my clothes on in a rush. He slid his feet in some slides, and he led me out the house. He opened my car door for me, and we were standing there as the awkward silence hung over us. I didn't want to assume anything, and I'm sure he didn't want to over talk. He pulled me into a tight embrace, and he backed away from me.

What the fuck just happened? I thought to myself.

I didn't have time to figure it out as I got in my car and sped home. Setting him up was going to be harder than I thought.

Cat Jenson

*I*nstead of being gone for the two weeks like I told Malice, I was only gone for a week and a half. A part of me told me that he had been fucking with someone else. The day I left, that dude was so out of it. I could tell that his mind was somewhere else. He would normally text me, but I hadn't gotten a text from him at all. Every time I text him, he told me that he was working. I knew that was a lie because I synced his calendar to my phone. Every time he added something to his calendar, it automatically synced to my calendar. He didn't know that I had done it. I wanted him to spend all his free time with me.

For as long as we have been fucking around, he has never lied to me about anything, as far as I know. Every time he tells me he is going somewhere, I would drive by there, and his car or motorcycle would be there. That didn't change until a few days ago. I texted him and asked him what he was doing, and he told me that he was cutting hair. As usual, I jumped in one of my less expensive cars, and drove past the place where he was cutting hair, and there was no one out there. I texted him again and asked him how long was he going to be cutting hair. He texted me and told me that he was going to be cutting hair for a few hours, and that he would hit me back when he was done. He never called. I felt my blood pressure rise to the ceiling. I was ready to go *Thin Line Between Love and Hate* on his ass.

I had been pacing my living room floor, smoking a cigarette. Smoking cigarettes calmed me down and kept me sane. If it wasn't for these things, I would have been killed some more people. Trying to hide this shit from Malice is getting harder and harder. He told me in the beginning that he hated cigarettes. The only time I smoke weed was with Malice, and that is when he was stressed about something. Weed makes me feel good as hell, and our sex is twenty times better when we are both high. I pulled out my phone and called Malice for the umpteenth time today, and he answered the phone on the second ring.

"What's up, Cat? You back?" he said into the phone like he hadn't been ignoring me all day.

"Yes, daddy! I'm back. I want to see you. I *need* to see you. Your favorite kitty misses you."

"Word! I'll slide through tonight. I'm busy right now."

"What are you busy doing?"

"Cat, I'm about to get on my motorcycle. I'll come by your place later. I promise," he said and hung up.

I was happy that he was on his motorcycle because it had a tracker in it, and I could track the last twenty places that his bike was at for over an hour. It's really such a good thing to have money. Checking his tracker, I could tell that he was moving now, so he wasn't lying about that. Out of the twenty places, I saw that he was at various hotels. I used my other phone to check his calendar, and it matched up perfectly. He drove his motorcycle to cut hair a few times. He went to his parents' home and school. Now, the rest of the places had Kam's Tees on it, and he was there each time after seven, and was there for hours. I know he bought some jerseys from that place, but there was no reason for him to be there every day for hours at a time.

Maybe he has a part-time job or something there, I thought to myself, then immediately shook that thought away. Malice told me after he quit his job at the hospital that he would never clock into no one else's job again, and he hasn't since he was sixteen years old, and he is almost thirty. Turning the fans on high and opening the windows, I was trying to get the smell out of here before Malice walked his sexy ass in here.

Waiting for Malice, I feel asleep until I felt something creeping up my thigh. I didn't even have to open my eyes to know that it was Malice because I smelled his cologne. It's crazy how a man could ride a motorcycle all day, and still smell good as hell. I opened my eyes and looked at the clock, and it was thirty minutes after midnight. I called him around six.

"Where you been? I called you six hours ago," I fussed.

"I had some business to handle. How was your trip?"

"My trip was good. I missed you the whole time. I wished that you could have come with me. Having to play with myself made me frustrated. So, what's been going on with you?"

"Nothing. You know, the usual. School and getting this paper," he replied.

I could see his silhouette from the light plug I had plugged in in the corner. I needed to see him, so I reached up and turned the lamp on. He was looking at me, and he was so handsome. I loved his short curly hair, and I loved running my fingers through it when he was between my legs. His beard was so fucking sexy. Watching him grow from a teenager to a man made me love him even more. I was with him when he didn't even have a beard.

"Getting the paper, huh? Can I ask you a question?"

"Yeah, what's up?"

"Would you ever lie to me?"

He shook his head before replying, "I really don't have a reason to lie to you, Cat. What do you think I've been lying to you about?"

"Are you fucking with other bitches other than the ones that pay you, and me? I mean, I know it's not any of my business, but I just want to know."

"Define fucking with. I met this cool chick, but am I fucking with her like that, nah. It's just some shit for my dad. That's all. Nothing more or nothing less," he said looking me in my eyes.

"Do you think about her when you are not with her? Has she been to your house? What is her name? Do you⬚"

"Cat, ma, you tweakin'. You asking me too many questions about shit that don't got shit to do with you. You just said that you know it's not your business, so why you spurt off all those questions? I don't know when you became this insecure person. You're not the same person that I met years ago."

"Malice, I been stopping my life for you, and⬚"

"Hol' up. Hol' up," he stood up. "Cat, ain't nobody told you to stop your life for me. Yeah, what we got is cool, but I ain't never told you to not go on a date. I encourage that sh…stuff for you. I want you to be happy. You deserve that."

That is not the answer that I wanted from him. I wanted him to say that he was happy for me stopping my life for him, and turning down dates for him. I get so many offers to go on dates, but I turned them down so I could be with Malice, but here he was, standing there breaking my heart. I hated myself for even crying because he was not moved by my tears.

"Malice, do you love me?" I asked as the tears flowed from my eyes.

He sat on the bed and wiped my tears away. He leaned forward, and I leaned back, thinking that he was getting ready to kiss me on my lips, but he kissed me on my forehead.

"Everything that you have done for me, Cat, how can I not have love for you. You put me on this money train, and I can't thank you enough for that. I'm not ready for no relationship type stuff. I'm trying to get my stuff together before I even think about getting in a relationship. You always tell me that you will take care of me, and you been doing that for the longest. I have to⬚"

"Malice, ever since your first client, you've been taking care of yourself. I just opened the door for you, and you've been making your own money. I just give you money because that's what I've been doing, and I ain't about to stop now. You still fuck me, and I still pay you. That's it. I don't ask you for your money because it's yours. You take care of me, and I take care of you," I said.

"Cat! Stop doing this, okay. It sounds like you are begging, and I don't like it. This is not you. Get yourself together."

I stared at him because something was different about him, but I just couldn't put my finger on it. I dried my tears up, laid back on the pillow, and stared at the ceiling.

"This is freaking crazy, Cat. Talk to me. I ain't know you felt this way about me. I swear I thought I was nothing more than just a play thing for you. Come on," he said, and placed his semi-cold hand on my stomach. I jumped at the touch of it.

"*Freaking* crazy. When did you start using a word like *freaking*?"

Looking in his face, I could tell that he was trying to hold back a smile, and I was confused.

"Just a little wager that I had with someone. No big deal, but I'm going to get out of here. I wanted to give you some dick, but you too emotional right now and I don't want to put you over the edge. I'll see you later, aight?"

"Whatever, Malice," I said, rolling my eyes.

"Don't be like that," he said.

He kissed my forehead and left me laying there seething. My body was hot from the way he just fucking curved me. I didn't even hear his motorcycle leave good before I cranked up my computer to do a search.

"Kam's Tees," I said to myself, as I typed the name into the search engine.

Within ten minutes, I pulled up everything about Ms. Kambridge Lewis. She was a beautiful twenty-two-year old black girl. She owned her own business. Graduated Magna Cum Laude from Northwestern

University, and even graduated valedictorian from the best private school in the whole state. Judge Kason is her daddy. I remember his fine ass. I stood many trials in front of him, and he would not cheat on his wife for nothing in the world.

"So, she comes from a good background," I mumbled to myself. "What can twenty-eight-year-old Malice do with this young broad? She can't provide him the life that I can, I don't care how much money her little store is making. The only social media she has is the one for her business page. So, I'm sure she is some quiet girl that thinks she wants a bad boy, but I'm going to have to let this little lady know that the bad boy she wants, is not Phoenix Bailey. I closed my computer and laid back down.

Malice had to be a fool to think that I was going to lose him to some young bitch, after I have spent years grooming him to be MINE! I thought to myself as I found my way to dreamland.

Kam

*T*oday was the last day of the two weeks, and I couldn't have been happier. Not wearing makeup, and wearing tank tops, showing more skin than I cared to, has taken a toll on me, but I can say it has made me just a little more comfortable with myself. I never thought that I would do such a thing. My family had been looking at me crazy for the last two weeks, leaving out the house with no makeup and shit, but I ain't want to tell them why I was doing it.

My dad called me in his office this morning, and asked me how was the thing with Malice going, and I told him that I was still working on it. I told him that I was working on getting him to trust me. Surprisingly, and I do mean, surprisingly, my dad has not laid a hand on me in two weeks, and that is HIGHLY unlike him. I almost wanted to ask him what was wrong with him. He even gave me a hug this morning. My dad has not hugged me since I don't know when. That's what I meant by when I said my dad was so hot and cold, but mostly hot.

Over the last two weeks, Malice and I had been getting very personal with each other. We'd been telling each other little things, but I still felt like he was holding back, as well as I was. I had gotten around to talking about his parents, but he told me that his mom is a homemaker, and says his dad owns a taxi company. That's it. That's all he says. He already knows about my parents, but that's it. We've been having so much fun just talking to each other, that I really ain't been having the chance to talk to him more about it.

Ever since that night that Malice made me squirt, that nigga been coming over here after hours, to first, make sure that I didn't have on makeup and that I had on a tank-top. Second, to stick his thick ass fingers inside of my vagina, to make me squirt. He seriously got off on making me squirt. He would come in, help me with a batch of shirts, and then when we were done, he put my ass on the table and stuck his fingers inside of me. I ain't never wanted dick so bad until I started fucking with him. He ain't never even let me see his dick, wouldn't even let me suck it, but he told me that I would be pleased with it.

My store was just opening, and in walked Connor's ass. I had forgiven him for saying 'nigga,' but I hadn't forgot about it. This was my first time seeing him in two weeks. We'd only been communicating by phone because I told him that I didn't want to see him just yet. Now that we were back talking, I know that it was going to be hard to keep Connor and Malice from finding out about each other, and I was such a horrible liar. Hopefully, they'd never run into each other.

"What do you have on?" Connor asked.

He had on a tailored suit, looking handsome as hell. If only Connor kept his mouth closed sometimes, he would be even finer. I braced myself for him to say something stupid.

"Good morning to you too, Connor," I replied.

"Seriously. I'm used to seeing you with no make-up, but you have your skin out," he said. "You know your scars are showing, right?" he whispered as if we weren't the only people in the room.

See, just like clockwork. I told you if he would just keep his mouth closed sometimes, we would be damn near perfect. I took a deep breath before I responded.

"Connor, I'm aware that my scars are showing. I put this on before I left the house. I'm sick of you slick making fun of my skin. You claim you *love* me, but only if I'm covered up. I'm only going to tell you this one last time, and if you bring it up again, I promise you, we will be done forever. Stop making fun of my skin. If you love me, you will love me regardless of what my skin looks like. Funny how you know how I got my scars, but instead of you telling me that I need to love myself, and you will help me love myself, you make me cover them up."

"Kambridge, I'm⌧"

"While we are talking, let me tell you something. This whole entire relationship has been about you. I could be having a bad day, and you *find* a way to make it about you, like your bad day is worse than my bad day. Connor, I am so sick of this shit. If I didn't love you so much I swear I would dump you, and never speak to you again in my life."

"Kambridge, I'm sorry. I never knew you felt⌧"

"Because you never took the time to listen to me. Every time I try to talk to you, you blow me off and start talking about your day."

"I'm sorry. I'm truly sorry. Whatever I can do to make it up to you, please let me know." He grabbed my hands and started kissing them both. "I don't want to lose you. You are my sun, earth, and moon."

I rolled my eyes at him, and before I could respond, he looked at his watch.

"Kam, can we please talk when I get off from work? We have to talk. I ain't letting you leave me, woman. You're so beautiful, I swear."

I nodded my head, and he left out of my store just as quick as he came. I knew Connor was just talking because I knew how he operates. I was getting my things together when my phone rung, and I already knew who it was because he had been calling me every morning for the last two weeks while he was on his way to class. I had finally given him my regular phone number.

"Kam's Tees," I answered.

"Hey, beautiful! How are you doing this morning?" Phoenix's deep voice vibrated my ear drums.

"I am doing fine. Just getting the store opened up, and before you ask, yes, I am still in tank-tops along with a bare face. I'm so glad today is the last day for this mess because *Kevyn Aucoin* and *Artis Fluenta* miss me," I said.

"Who the feezy is them niggas?" he asked.

I laughed because he had been using 'feezy' instead of the word fuck, and it was so funny to me. I am so proud of him because he had gone from cursing three times in one sentence to not at all, and he promised me that he hadn't been cursing at all, and for some odd reason, I believed him.

"Kam, I ain't laughing, lil' girl. Who are they?"

"*Kevyn* and *Artis* are my very expensive makeup brushes. They haven't felt my skin in two weeks, and I know they are calling out to me," I laughed.

"How much them brushes run you? I ain't trying to be in your pockets or nothing. I just want to know how much you paying for something you *don't* need."

"You trying to trick me. Don't be trying to buy your lil' girlfriends none of my brushes. They wouldn't know what to do with them."

"Mane, tell me how much they cost!"

"*Kevyn's* brushes were a little over seven hundred dollars after tax, and *Artis's* brushes were a little over five hundred dollars after tax."

Sccccrrrrrreeecchh.

I heard tires squealing and horns honking in Phoenix's background then silence. My heart started thumping because I thought he had a car accident or something.

"Phoenix, are you there?" I whispered.

"Hooollllll' the freak up! You paying over a thousand dollars for some freaking brushes? I had to pull over and make sure I heard you correctly. Aw, heck naw! If I had a girl, I wish she would muster the energy to ask me to pay over a thousand dollars for some freaking makeup brushes. Mane, I can go cut some dang hair off a horse and make a brush fo' yo' tail."

"Imagine a grown woman mustering the energy to ask a man anything," I said and laughed.

"Your mouth is so smart, but I got something for that. Just wait on it."

My door chimed letting me know that someone had walked in. I looked up, and it was a white woman that I had never seen before. She was walking to the counter, so I had to rush Phoenix off the phone.

"Hey, I have to let you go because I have a customer at the counter. Will you be coming by tonight?"

"You don't have to ask. Yes, I'm taking you somewhere for committing to the two weeks with minimum complaining. So, go grab you something to wear on your lunch break, and you can shower at my house since it's closer to your shop than your house is. Alright. Blow me a kiss. I need it. Got a test today."

"Good luck!" I said, and made kissy noises into the phone.

After I hung up the phone, I smiled to myself, but got a really weird look from this white lady who was now eye balling me.

"Sorry about that. Good friend of mine is a real goofball. How can I help you?"

"He doesn't sound like just a friend the way that he has you smiling over there. If you were my color, your face would be red," she said.

"No, he's really a good friend. Scouts honor. How can I help you?" I asked again.

"Um, I'm not sure. What all do you have?"

"Depends on what you are looking for. I can put your logo on anything including cups, shirts, hats, jerseys, pens, tablecloths, purses, and backpacks. I'm working on getting an embroidery machine in here so I can stitch initials into t-shirts as well. Anything I said interest you?

What's your name, you are such a beautiful woman?" I asked, trying to turn down the level of awkwardness I was feeling because of the way she was gawking at me.

"Yes. I'm interested in getting a t-shirt. Can I get it within an hour or so? I'll be going across the street to the boutique. My name is Catherine Jenson. I just want something simple on a t-shirt, and I want it to say the letters 'P. M. B.' and then put 'is mine.' The colors can be black and white, and can you a picture of a black man and a white woman on it. Do you have all of that?"

"Yes, ma'am! I think I do. What size shirt do you need?"

"I think I may need a medium. How much will it be?"

"For this, it will be fifteen dollars."

When I told her the price, she had a shocked look on her face. I swiped her card and told her to sign the receipt.

"Um, if I may get in your business, how do you make money charging fifteen dollars a shirt? Your store looks pretty dead in here to be charging that little for a t-shirt."

"Well, Mrs. Jenson, you did get in my business a little, but I have been opened since I graduated from college, so my fifteen dollars a shirt is reasonable. Also, if you must know, I get several large orders online, and every other day, which can easily be a thousand dollars in one day. Large corporations order things from me for their business, which is maybe five to ten thousand dollars, and especially when they have those large conferences that last a week or so. So, my business is doing well. Next time you try to clock someone's pockets, don't. I'll have your shirt in an hour," I said, ending the conversation.

After her snatching her thin blond edges for trying to come for my store, she scurried out my store with the quickness. I made her logo online, and had her shirt done within thirty minutes. I guess I was working under pressure because she had me hotter than a firecracker.

An hour later, she walked back in the store, and I already had her shirt ready for her. Hopefully she'd just pick her damn shirt up and walk out. When she made it to the counter, I stood up to hand her the shirt, but then she started talking.

"Hello, I wanted to apologize for how I came at you earlier," she said.

I looked up at the door, and Shelly's ass was walking in, looking like a model.

"It's okay."

She asked me what I had planned for tonight, and I stared at her like she had two heads on her shoulders. This woman literally just came for my neck not too long ago, now she trying to act like we were friends. I looked past her and at Shelly, who was pointing at her and mouthing 'who is this white bitch'? I smirked at her, and continued to ignore the woman asking me personal questions about my life, until she apologized again and walked out of the store.

"Girl, who was that white bitch all in your damn business? You better than me because I would have cursed her out," Shelly said, walking behind the counter and taking a seat next to me.

"Girl, I don't know. She came in here, bought a shirt, and then tried to read me about my damn store. Girl, you know I let her have it. What's been up?"

"Not shit. You ain't fucked with me in two weeks. Where you been? You look pretty hot without makeup, you know that, right? But what happened to your back and your arms? Don't give me a bull shit story either. I've noticed them before, but I ain't say nothing. Spill it."

She made me smile with her comment. You know how a man can tell you something and you don't believe it, but when your GIRL tells you the same stuff, you believe it without second thought? That's kind of how I feel right now. I was hyped up.

"Um, only if you promise to tell me why you and Connor hate each other so much," I said, taking a sip of my water.

"Bitch, because I fuck his daddy from time to time. He has caught me riding his daddy's dick one too many times," she said nonchalantly, making me choke on my water. She literally had to pat me on my back.

"How... I mean why?"

"It's thick, and he knows what he is doing with it. Now, about you."

Now I see why people be wondering how me and Shelly are friends. This girl doesn't care about nothing. I can't wait until the day that I am that carefree.

"Shelly, promise me that you won't say anything about what I'm about to tell you. Promise me. If you tell anyone, I swear I will murder you."

"Damn, girl! I promise. All your secrets have been safe with me. Not that have you many, but they are safe."

I took a deep breath and told her everything about my father beating me, sending me to the hospital several times, and even what happened the night she left me stranded in the club while she got a train ran on her. I told her what he wanted me to do with Malice and how he wants me to get the information. I had been walking around holding these secrets in, and for once, I felt relieved when I told someone about them. I even let her in on what Malice had been doing to me every damn night for the last two weeks. When I was finished, she sat there with her mouth formed into a big 'O' and then she started crying. This was weird to me because I had never seen her cry before.

"Shelly, say something," I urged.

"I am so sorry that this happened to you. Why didn't you tell me? We could have been murdered your father, and they would have never found his body. My parents love you, they would have loved to have taken you in. Furthermore, I always knew your dad was weird. You should see the way he looks at you sometimes. When I used to come over your house a lot, I wanted to ask if you were okay, but I figured if you weren't you would have told me," she said through her tears. "Don't ever keep another secret away from me," she said, swatting at my arm.

"I'm sorry, girl. I won't keep another secret from you," I said.

"Good. Now that we got all that shit out, girl, you better not let that crazy nigga find out what you trying to do because that nigga will kill you. His last name is fucking Bailey. Bailey boys will riddle you with bullets and then ask for an explanation. Anyways, get out of here and go get you a little outfit to wear. I will cover the store for a little while.

∞

Phoenix and I were sitting in this nice expensive restaurant. It was two levels, and the lights were low. We were sitting on the top level and had a good view of the bottom floor. I had bought me a black glitter deep V-neck bodycon dress, and I paired it with a pair of gold studded Valentino heels that I had in my trunk. My trunk is another closet for me. Phoenix had on a black button down along with a pair of black chinos, and some nice shoes. I don't know what they were, but they looked expensive. He had a black bow tie laid around his neck instead of having it tied. He was looking so fine.

"Dang, baby girl, I'm sorry to hear that," he said, rubbing my hand.

I had just finished telling him about the white lady that tried me today in my store. I had even forgot her name, and didn't even care to remember it.

"It's alright. Thank you for treating me to dinner. I have never heard of this place before."

"Mane, I ain't never ate here before either, but I saw it had good reviews on the internet, so I chose it. Secluded and has a great atmosphere. Do you drink? They have a list of great wines here."

"I haven't had a drink before, but after these last two weeks, I think I could use one. You pick a wine and I'll drink it."

The waiter approached the table, took our orders, and disappeared just as quick as he came. I hadn't been on a date in so long that I didn't even know what to say.

"Penny for your thoughts?"

"Um, this feels weird to me. I haven't been on a date in so long to the point where I don't even know what to ask or what to say. You look good tonight, though. I ain't even know you could clean yourself up like this, but anyways, how was your test today?"

"Don't hype me up like that, Kambridge, but it was good. I did better than I expected, considering that I didn't really study for it. You look beautiful tonight as well. You know what's more attractive to me than your beautiful black ass skin, and your beautiful smile? Your mind, Kambridge. Your mind set is sexy as heck, man. At twenty-two, all that you have accomplished, I'm jealous of that. At twenty-two, I was just barely getting my GED."

"It wasn't easy, I can tell you that much, but it doesn't matter where or how you start, as long as you start and finish. Accomplish all the goals that you set for yourself. At least you are more than what the statistics say. The statistics say that you were supposed to be a drug dealer, dead, or in jail, but you are neither. Congrats to that," I said, and lifted the glass that the waiter had just set on the table.

We tapped glasses and took a sip. The sip was strong at first, but it tasted good. Our food looked good as well, and you could tell that it was an expensive restaurant because the food was small on our plate. I took a bite of my chicken, and it was so good that it damn near melted in my mouth.

"Thank you, Kambridge," he randomly said.

"For what?" I asked, looking up at him.

"Um, for not wearing makeup and wearing your skin out. I know how hard it is for you to show your skin, but I must let you know that you look good as heck to me, man. You don't need that. I know you getting tired of me saying that, but it's true."

He had me smiling from ear to ear like a little girl. I went in my purse because I had something for him as well. He was going to be in for a lovely surprise when he saw it. I slid him the envelope and watched him open it. I had purchased him two tickets to St. Maarten, and it was a passport. I stole one of his pictures from the internet and had him a passport made. I know a few people who could make it look like he purchased it a year ago because you have to have had your passport for at least six months.

"Nah, Kam! How were you able to do this? This has the seal on it and everything. St. Maarten. Mane, I ain't never heard of this place in my life, nor have I been on a plane. You ain't have to do this for me. I swear you didn't. Hell, you got two tickets for me, why don't we just go together?"

"I mean, I wasn't expecting… wow. I mean, I guess we can," I replied, but I was happy as hell on the inside. I knew what I was doing when I bought the tickets.

We ate in silence, and I was looking all over the restaurant when I saw Connor and Holly sitting comfortable in a booth looking like a happy couple. A part of me wanted to go act a fool, but I couldn't because I'm with another nigga, and they didn't need to find out about each other. He wanted to play games, then I can play games with him as well. I smiled to myself.

"What you over there smiling for, woman?"

"No reason. Just thinking about how happy I am at this exact moment."

"Kambridge, this is going to be very straightforward, and please let me know if I am out of line. I want to make love to you. I know what you said about you wanting to give your virginity to your husband, but I… you just make me feel things that I haven't felt before, and I don't know…this seems crazy to me. I ain't never had to ask for pussy. My fault, but you know."

"That was very straightforward, but yes, you…that's her," I said as my eyes danced around to the bottom level again.

He turned around and replied, "That's who?"

"The white lady who tried me in my store. She is even wearing the shirt that I made for her today. Catherine. That's her name," I said rolling my eyes.

His jaws started clenching, and I touched his hand. He looked back at me.

"Phoenix, are you okay? You look really pissed. You know her or something?" I asked.

"Nah, I just wanna go say something to her for fucking with you today. That's all. Let me pay the check so I can take you to my house, so I can… you know. I heard your answer." He winked at me.

He paid the check and we left the restaurant. The car ride was quiet until he put his hand on my thigh and started rubbing his hand up my leg, touching the outside of my thong. I put my hand on top of his and started helping him rub my throbbing pussy.

"Turn this way and let me see it, baby," he whispered.

"Phoenix, you are driving. We can't⬚"

"The fuck did I say?"

My pussy started throbbing at his request. A part of me missed that part of him because it turned me on. I rolled my dress up and turned to the side. One leg was behind his seat, and the other leg was on the dashboard. My bare ass was on his leather seats, feeling good to my ass. He turned the light on and then stuck his fingers inside of me.

"Phhooeexnix, you are driving, ahh."

"I know, fuck, and you are wet as hell," he whispered.

I watched through hooded eyes, as Phoenix paid attention to the road and me at the same time.

"Oooowwee, Phoenixxx, baby!"

"Give it to me, Kam. Fuck these seats up. Daddy can get these seats cleaned. Fuck 'em up, mama," he spoke as he continued to push his fingers inside of me and push on my g-spot.

"Ahhh, fuuckkkk!"

My juices squirted all over his seats, and a little bit got on him. He kept rubbing his hands up and down my sensitive pussy. I felt the car coming to a stop, and I could see streetlights so that meant we were not on his road. I raised up and this nigga had pulled over on side of the road.

"Sit up," he ordered.

I sat up and he let his seat all the way back.

"Come here," he whispered huskily.

"You are not about to penetrate me in this car."

"I know, so get yo' ass over here."

I climbed over the armrest and got on top of him. Phoenix gripped the bottom of my thighs and slid me up to his face. All I could do was hold on to the backseat's headrest, while Phoenix devoured my pussy. He gripped my ass cheeks while he played with my clit with his tongue.

SMACK!

He smacked my ass while he moaned into my pussy, sending me over the edge.

"Phoenixxxxxx, oh my Gooodddddd. I'm cumming!" I screamed out as I rode his face.

He slid me down, and I didn't have much strength to move. He let the seat up and pulled back out into the highway with me on top of him.

"Lil' mama, you taste good as fuck. Mane, I'm about to fuck the shit out of you, shorty, and you don't even know it," he whispered before he kissed my forehead.

We drove for a few more minutes before he pulled into his garage. He opened the door and stepped out with me still on him. He picked me up, got his balance, and carried me in the house.

"You are much stronger than you look." I grinned as he threw me on his bed.

He grabbed my dress and pulled it over my head, leaving me in nothing but my thong. He slid me to the edge of the bed, got on his knees, pulled my thong to the side, and buried his face between my legs. It felt so fucking good. He hooked my legs over his shoulders and stuck his tongue deep inside of my hole. I grabbed the back of his head, and held it in place.

"Phoenix," I moaned his name, as I released in his mouth.

He came up with my juices coating his lips, and even in his beard. He got undressed slowly, his eyes never leaving mine. He laid on top of me, staring me deep into my eyes.

"Can I kiss you, Phoenix?"

Reluctantly, he nodded his head. I grabbed the back of his head and brought him to my mouth. I loved to kiss, so I pushed my tongue in his mouth and danced around with his. I bit his bottom lip and then sucked on it. I latched onto his tongue, and started sucking my juices off tongue. I pulled back, and that nigga's face was red. He was looking at me like I was his first kiss or something.

"Fuck, Kam," he groaned before he took one of my nipples in his mouth.

He was going back and forth between each nipple at a rapid pace, turning my body heat up. He came back up and looked me in my eyes with a very intense glare. I swallowed hard because I knew what was about to happen. He sat up on his knees and grabbed my right hand, and placed it on his rock-hard abs.

"Kam, nothing about this first few minutes is going to be nice, or pleasurable, but you stop me whenever it gets to be too much. You push me back whenever it starts to hurt too much, okay?"

I nodded my head, and he positioned himself at my throbbing wet opening, and pushed the head of his dick inside of me. He put his right hand over mine, leaned over, tucking his arm under my back. He pushed more inside of me, and I gasped at the pain.

"Ssssss." He hissed as he bit down on my shoulder blade. "Stop me, Kam, if I'm hurting you," he whispered, and then bit down on my neck. He pushed more inside of me, and I had to stop him, and he pulled out. He placed his lips on mine, and the way he was breathing against my lips did something to me.

"Put it back in, baby. I want it all," I whispered, after I placed my hand on his face.

He put it back in me and pushed in more than before. I was moaning in pain, so he placed my hand back on his abs, I guess so I could let him know if I need him to stop again.

"Kam, another inch and I'll be all the way in," he whispered huskily, before he thrust all the way of the way inside of me, and I yelped out in pain.

"Shh! Shh! It's alright. I'm right here. I ain't never letting you go," he whispered while staring in my eyes. "You hear how wet you are. This pussy feel so good, Kambridge."

He started going in and out of me slowly. The strokes felt so good to the point where tears were sliding down the sides of my face.

"Phoeenixx, baby. Oh my God! Don't stop!" I whimpered.

"Fuck!" he grunted, pulled out of me, and nutted on my pussy lips. "This shit so fucking beautiful."

He played with my clit with the head of his dick, spreading his nut all over the place, and then pushed back inside of me. Phoenix wrapped my arms around his neck and stood up. He had full control as he slid me up and down on his thick dick. I tried to avoid his eye contact, but it was no use as he demanded that I look him directly into his eyes.

"Kam, tell me…tell me why you crying, baby?"

"This feels so good! I never imagined…ah, I'm cumming, baby."

"I feel you running down my leg. This shit feels so good, baby. Fuck! Damn, please don't let this be the only time I get this. Ohh shit! Lil' mama, I'm about to nut again."

He thrust inside me one more time, before pulling out and getting nut on both of us. He laid me on the bed, and fell on the side of me, trying to catch his breath. Is this what love felt like? Being completely naked? Trusting someone with something so precious like your virginity? Being able to share some of your deepest darkest secrets with them? Your fantasies. Your hopes, and dreams. The harsh reality. Phoenix has given me all that plus more since the day he walked into my store. I loved him.

After I told myself the truth, I immediately burst into tears because I wasn't supposed to fall in love with him. I got up and started gathering my things while crying like a baby.

"Kam, what's going on? Talk to me. Why you crying like that? Did you not want to do it? I'm sorry for whatever I did. Kam, please stop crying, man. What happened?" he said, trying to get in his clothes.

Phoenix fired off question after question while I got dressed, and rushed out of his room and out the front door. He was hot on my heels, but I was able to get in my car door and shut it. He pulled on the handle, but I figured I owed him some type of explanation. I put a crack in the window.

"I'm sorry, we shouldn't have done that. I'm so sorry," I cried and backed out of the driveway, leaving him standing there with his hands clasped together on top of his head.

While driving, I blocked him from both of my phones, and then I called Kade. He answered the phone on the first ring.

"What's happening, baby sis?"

"Kade! We did it! I did it! I feel so stupid," I sobbed. "I gave him my virginity because I love him, and I wasn't supposed to fall in love with him. I don't know what to do. I blocked him from my phones. I can't talk to him anymore. This isn't right. What we have isn't real. Everything was built on a lie."

"Kam, calm down. I'll be home in two minutes. Where are you?"

"Turning the corner now," I said and hung up the phone.

Kade and I pulled in the gate basically at the same time. As soon as we both exited our cars, I fell into his arms and cried like a baby, while my brother patted my back, letting me know that everything was going to be okay.

Malice

That fuck shit with Kambridge had me on edge all fucking week. The only thing I could do to take my mind off that black ass girl was to double up on clients all fucking week. A nigga made close to forty thousand dollars this week. That stupid mothafucka ain't even been to her fucking store all week. Every time I stopped in there, Shelly's stupid ass was working her store. She had me so fucked up to the point where I ain't been to class all week. I had to send an email to my professors telling them that I have meningitis. You know you can't go to class with that shit because it's contagious.

Every time I close my fucking eyes, it's like I feel myself slowly opening her up vagina walls. I feel myself kissing her lips and her biting my tongue. When I lick my lips, it's like I taste the remnants of her pussy juices on them. Nibbling on her pussy lips made my dick the hardest it had ever been, and I've been fucking for a long time. She ruined me and I know it. I hate that I can't stop thinking about her. She opened her mind, body, and soul to me, and so did I. I never dreamed that I would be kissing, sucking, and fucking on a woman as beautiful as Kambridge. Everything with her came natural, that's why I gave her all of me, raw. She was mine. I had her just where I wanted her, and she slipped right through my fingers, with no explanation of why except *'we shouldn't have done this'*. Watching her cry like that hurt my soul for real. Every time I picked up the phone to call her, I remembered that she had me blocked from everything.

Looking at my phone ring, it was Cat calling for the two hundredth time this week. Don't even get me started on her sheisty ass. I didn't even know how the fuck she knew about Kam, but for her to go in there and get my initials and shit on a shirt, and then wear it out? My poor baby didn't even realize it, and I was thankful. I know she couldn't have, because Kam wouldn't have fucked me if she knew that. She left voicemail after voicemail, but I was straight deleting them, not even listening to them.

"Tsk, tsk, tsk... look at you. Out here sulking. I told you to leave that girl alone, now look at you," Mayhem said, coming out on the rooftop. "Here, you need this more than me," he said, handing me a blunt.

"Mane, how you know I even fucked with her like that?" I asked him as I lit the blunt, and puffed it.

"I heard her moaning and shit. She sounded good as fuck," he said, and I shot him a look. "All I was doing was going on the roof to smoke, and I walked by the room. You were making love to her, and now your feelings hurt. What did big bro tell you?"

"Pryor, come on, man, damn! I don't know what happened. We were...whatever we were doing,⊠"

"Making love, fam," he laughed. "Say it. You'll feel better."

"Making love, damn, you happy? I was kissing all over her body, doing some of my best work, and when we were finished, she laid there for a second and burst into tears. Bro, she would not tell me what was wrong. She just cried. I chased her to the car, and she said that we shouldn't have done that. She dipped out, and I haven't heard from her or seen her since. She ain't even been in her store. Her lil' white friend was in there."

"Damn, bro. You really feeling her, ain't you? What you gon' tell your daddy when he asks about his damn gold again?"

"Man, I honestly haven't even been thinking about that. When I'm with her, we just laugh and click. She even wanna be a business partner when I finish school, and it don't sound like a bad idea. But peep this, you know Cat know about Kam. I been avoiding her because if I get close to her, I'll probably choke the fuck out of her. She went to Kam's shop, got a shirt made with my initials, and then showed up to the damn restaurant where we were eating. I was pissed. You know how hard it was to keep my composure while sitting there?"

"Damn, bro! All this stemming from you not listening to what the fuck I told you. I told you not to fuck with that girl on that level, and now you got a shit storm brewing. You continue to fuck with this girl and that may mess up your main money flow, because you know Cat got influence around this bitch. All them old bitches will stop fucking with you, or you tell Kam how you get money, and she leaves you alone. She probably will anyway because if you keep fucking with her… Cat ain't gon' leave y'all alone. So, either way, it seems you like fucked." Mayhem put things in perspective for me.

I was getting ready to respond when my phone went off again. It was another text message from Cat. I was leaving her bitch ass on read because she was playing games with me. I opened the message.

*Cat: *1 video attached. Keep fucking ignoring me, and I will let this lil bitch know everything about you. She don't know you like I do. You think a smart girl like that will take a male escort home to her parents.*

My nostrils flared as I watched a video of her, Kade, and another little girl, who must be their little sister, Kalena, out eating. I could tell that they were trying to cheer her up because she looked sad. In a way, I was happy that she was feeling the way that I was feeling. Sick. I showed Mayhem the video, and he shook his head.

"This is going to get very ugly, bro, very," my brother said, shaking his head.

The minute my phone rung and it was Cat, I picked it up before it could ring a second time.

"Why the fuck are you playing games?" I roared into the phone.

"Games...? What's games? You ain't seen games," she said and hung up the phone.

I squeezed my phone, tapping it against my head to think. This woman had me frustrated to my fucking core.

"I'll be back," I said to my brother.

"Yo, go see your dad too, ASAP," he said to my back.

I jumped in my car and weaved through traffic to get to Cat's house. When I got there, I used my key to get in, and the minute she walked out the kitchen, I yanked her off her feet by her throat.

"Yo, why are you fucking playing with me?" I spoke through gritted teeth while she clawed at my fingers.

"Mal... Mal..." she tried to choke out, but I squeezed harder.

Just when she was getting ready to pass out, I threw her down to the ground. She started scooting back like I was getting ready to do some more damage to her. My handprint around her neck was already red and now turning purple. I really wasn't thinking because this bitch could end me at any moment. She started crying real tears, but I didn't feel bad.

"Cat, why you fucking playing with me, man? You showing up to my girl☒"

"YOUR GIRL!" she cried out while clenching her stomach.

Kam wasn't really my girl, and it felt weird as fuck saying that. I guess in my mind after how far we've come, I guess I considered her my girl.

"AFTER EVERYTHING I HAVE DONE FOR YOU! I MADE YOU THE MOST MONEY THAT YOU WOULD HAVE EVER MADE. *I* DID THAT, *NOT* HER! HOW COULD YOU DO THAT TO ME?" she screamed out in pain.

"Look, Catherine. We have discussed this before, ma. I never asked you to stop your life, ever. This shit with her just feels different than what you and I have. She gets me, and I get her. It's nothing personal. It's not like I went looking for this, it just happened right in front of my eyes."

"You really have feelings for her." She looked up at me with a red face and puffy eyes. "Have you fucked her?"

"Why you ask a question that you really don't want to know the answer to?"

"DID YOU!" she screamed.

"Yeah, I did."

"HOW! HOW DID YOU FUCK HER? DID YOU USE A CONDOM LIKE YOU DO WITH ME? DID YOU KISS HER? DID YOU EAT HER PUSSY?"

"Cat, I'm going to go. Um, I don't know where this leaves us, but if you want to call me then do so."

She jumped up and pushed herself up against me. Wrapping her arms around my neck, she tried to kiss me in my mouth, but I kept dodging it and she kept landing on my neck.

"Malice, we can work this out. We have history. That little relationship or whatever ain't got shit on twelve years. I forgive you. Please just say you'll leave her alone," she pleaded.

I grabbed her by her wrists and pried her arms from around my neck. She took a seat on the couch, looking at me with puppy dog eyes.

"Look, we will always be friends. I owe you that, but a relationship between us will probably never happen. Deep down, you know you couldn't be with me like that. You took me to your galas, but that's as far as it goes with us. I want to get married one day, and you know that if you want to keep your influences with those other white people, you wouldn't dare let me put a ring on your finger. You couldn't dare marry me. Not only am I two decades younger than you, but I'm also black. You would lose your clout before you could even say 'I do'. You sitting right there with that stupid look on your face because you know it's true. Now, like I said before, I will always be your friend, but a relationship will never happen."

She didn't say anything at all. I'm assuming that she was processing what I was saying. After like five minutes of non-stop crying, she looked up at me with venom in her eyes.

"Does she know?" she seethed, as her chest heaved up and down like a dragon getting ready to spit fire.

"Cat--"

"Does...she...know? Answer me!"

"Nah, and I prefer to keep it that way."

She gave me a weird flat smile. A smile that said that she had some shit up her sleeve. A smile that I knew was going to have some bullshit behind it.

"Hmm, well..." She stood up and flattened her skirt out. "A wise man once said, oh what a tangled web we weave when first we practice to deceive," she grinned. "Have a good day, Malice!"

We gave each other a long hard stare before I turned to exit her home. I got in my car and left with no particular destination in mind. Earlier, I got Kade's number from my brother, and decided to give him a call. He answered after the third ring.

"Kade Lewis," he spoke into the phone.

"*Kade Lewis,* ol' mark ass, prep school ass nigga. Listen, this Malice. Where yo' sister? I need to see her," I said.

"How are you going to call me, insult me, then ask me something? You need me to chin check you again?"

"My nigga, if you ever get a lick off me like that again, you won't live to tell nobody else about it. Where your sister?"

"She's in the Tropical Smoothie, getting a smoothie for us."

"That's some prep school shit. Who the fuck drinks smoothies? Can you bring her to the mall? I really need to see her, mane. I ain't never begged nobody for shit, but I really need to see her. I need her to tell me face to face that she don't want to fuck with me no more."

"Look, I really don't want to get in my sister's☒"

"NIGGA, FUCK THAT! You inserted yourself in this shit when you snuffed me in my jaw. Bring her to the mall. I don't want to come find you. I'll be on the top-level parking deck. Bye!" I hung up the phone before he could protest.

Kambridge

inding out I loved someone, finding out my boyfriend is really cheating on me, and having to stop fucking with them both, all in the same week was hard. I had been avoiding them both, putting them both on the block list, but it had done nothing for my sanity. Every time I closed my eyes, I thought about having sex with Malice. He shouldn't have looked at me the way he was looking, or touching and rubbing all over me like he really cared about me. We would have probably been fine, but he was making love to my mind, body, and soul.

That night, I cried in Kade's arms for like an hour before I could talk about the way I was feeling about Phoenix. I told him that what we had was built on a lie because I was talking to him under false pretenses. I was only talking to him because of my dad. Nothing more, or nothing less, and then he got inside of mind and made me very vulnerable to him. Kade said that those are natural reactions when you love someone. He also made me realize that just because our dad was on some crazy shit doesn't mean I really don't love Malice. He told me that everything happens for a reason, and that it was a reason I saw Connor and Holly in that restaurant. He told me that it was a sign that I needed to leave Connor's lying ass alone, and that's what I'm going to do.

I had Shelly working at my store because I knew that he would come by my store. Shelly would text me after he left so I could come in and do the orders, then slide right back out without him seeing me. Connor's ass was so easy to ignore, despite me feeling like this whole relationship was a lie. I guess he realized he was on the block list and started sending me emails. He was asking me why I wasn't picking up the phone for him, and he even came by the house once. I told him that I didn't feel like hearing from him, and that he should go and talk to Holly. He kept asking me what I was talking about. Connor lied right down to the end, and then he finally admitted it. After he admitted it, he said that it wasn't nothing special, and that they were talking about work. I told him you don't take a bitch there to *talk about work*. Phoenix didn't think I noticed, but that bill was over four hundred dollars, so ain't no telling how much they spent.

Walking outside of Tropical Smoothie, I saw Kade on the phone, and then he hung up immediately when he saw me.

"Who were you on the phone with? Or is that any of my business?" I asked getting in the car.

"Um, your boy. He wanna see you, and he doesn't want to come find us."

"Phoenix. That sounds like him. I can't avoid him forever. Just take me to him," I sighed.

"You don't have to see him if you don't want to. You do know that, right?"

"Yeah, I know, but it just seems easier to say what I have to say face to face."

"Mane, you just want to see him. You ain't got to lie to kick it with me," he laughed.

I laid the seat back and sipped on my smoothie until we pulled up at the mall. We made it to the top level of the parking deck, and my heart started beating fast as fuck when I saw Malice leaning against his car, smoking. He had on one of his jerseys with his chest and abs on full display. He had on a pair of black jeans, along with a pair of black and white Jordans. He really was fine as hell.

"Dang, sis! Is that the guy that's been sweating you? He is so fine. Connor don't look nearly as good as him. Get out and go talk to him," Kalena said.

"Girl, he ain't *that* good looking," I lied. "You hype him up, you may never hear the end of it."

I got out the car and walked slowly over to him, leaning against the passenger side of his car. He stared at me as he was inhaling his blunt. I know that he was frustrated because he told me he only smoked when he was stressed. As soon as I stepped in his face, he blew the smoke in my face. I coughed while waving the smoke out of my face.

"How much have you smoked?" I asked, trying to ease myself into this conversation.

"Two or three a day since you left my house in tears. Haven't been to school. Didn't know you cared since you been ducking and dodging me for the last week," he said and pushed himself off the car, and started pacing in front of me. "You fucked with my head, all for you to play some type of game with me. What the fuck type of shit you on?"

I felt myself getting ready to tear up again. My eyes darted to the ground, while I clenched myself like I was cold.

"Look at me when I'm fucking talking to you," he growled.

My pussy tingled at the roar of his voice. I looked up at him, and I could see his jaws clenching like he was extremely mad.

"Matter of fact, get the fuck in the car," he said while opening the door.

I got in the car, and he slammed the door. I looked a few parking spaces down at Kade's car. When he got in the car, we stared at each other, before he leaned in and started kissing me so passionately. He pushed his tongue in my mouth, damn near making me swallow it. He was making my pussy get wet, and I had on a thong, so I tried to pull away, but he gripped the back of my neck, keeping me right where he wanted me. He continued to assault my mouth with his, and I was getting weaker and weaker.

"I missed you, man. Talk to me. Why the fuck you bounce out on me like that?" he whispered against my lips.

Sighing, I replied, "I don't know. Just thought you only wanted one thing, and I⌧"

"Kambridge--" he cut me off, but I continued.

"I was ashamed that I gave you my virginity after barely knowing you when... I felt so much like a slut, that I had started to like you, and I know you don't feel that way about me, especially after giving it up so soon. I don't know." I shrugged.

"Kambridge, you ain't even stay to ask. You just took off and ignored me for what seems like forever, man. But if you must know, I think you are a beautiful young woman, and you have a kind heart. There is no way that I could *not* like you. It's not the sex. Trust me."

"So, what are you saying to me, Phoenix?" I sat back against the window and looked into his face.

"We can kick it until we are both ready to make this official, but it's all up to you though. Let me make something clear. DO YOU! I ain't in no way, shape, form, or fashion, trying to stop your life. If you want to date other people…do that! As long as when daddy call, you fucking come. Are we clear?"

"That is a high demand. What about you? If you are on a date, are you going to come when I call?" I asked while rolling my neck.

"Anything for you my beautiful black queen," he said, and rubbed his hand along my jawline. "So, what have you been doing for the last week since you've been ignoring me? When do you go to your shop because you truly avoided me like the plague?" he chuckled.

"Well, I knew you would stop by, so I had Shelly working there for me. She ain't got shit else to do," I said as Malice started inching his hand up my dress, making me swallow hard. "Um, when you would leave, I would go in really quickly, do an…an order, and then leave out really fast. I couldn't… ahhh, fuck!" I moaned in the middle of my sentence when he pushed his finger inside of my wet pussy. "That's it… um, hmmmm, shit. Um, play my violin, and I… made a pottery vase from my mom's pottery things. That's…that's it."

"Did you miss this?"

I nodded my head because that's all I could do. My voice was caught in my throat because I had thought about this feeling since last week. He let his seat back as he kept the pace with finger fucking me. He unzipped his pants and pulled out his dick. I licked my lips at the sight of it. I didn't get a good look at it when we fucked the first time, but now that I'm looking at it, it's so fucking cute. A thick zig zag vein going from side to side down to the middle. Phoenix started stroking himself, and I could see the pre-cum ooze out his head.

"All of that was inside of me?" I whispered. "Whhyyy are you such a fucking good multi-tasker?"

"Yes, you took it like a champ. I'm proud of you. You like that I'm a multitasker. Do you want to sit on it?"

My eyes bucked at that question because I wasn't expecting to sit on that. My heart started to quicken at the thought of him stretching me open again.

"Come here, Kambridge Lewis," he whispered. "He misses you."

I looked at his dick, and he made it jump, in turn making me giggle like a schoolgirl. After hesitating for too long, he grabbed me by my arm and pulled me across the seat. He immediately ripped my thong off and placed it in his cup holder. Placing my knees comfortably on each side of his legs, straddling him, I placed his dick at my opening, and slid halfway down on it.

"Fuck!" I groaned.

"I'm rubbing off on you. You been cursing up a storm," he laughed at me.

"That's why I gotta stop fucking with your black ass." I laughed at myself for cursing again.

I started going up and down on his dick slowly. He laid his head back on his headrest, but kept his eyes planted on me. He pulled his bottom lip in his mouth before he let out a moan. Placing both of my hands on his for leverage, I started speeding up.

"Phoenixxx," I moaned.

"What's up, mama? You love that dick?"

I leaned my head back from the pleasure that I was feeling up and through my body. Phoenix caught me off guard when he grabbed my chin tight, placing the tip of his index finger in my mouth.

"Ooowwee, it's so much dick in me. Why you got it all in there like thiisss? Malice, oh my Gooodddd!"

"Ma, you controlling everything you feel right now. I'm just enjoying it."

He took that index finger that was in my mouth, and started rubbing my clit so fast that I started bouncing up and down on his dick like I wasn't an amateur.

"Daddddyy, I'm getting ready to… oooweee, shhitttt!"

"Come on, ma! Daddy finna give you all this shit," he growled.

He grabbed onto my waist and started bouncing me even harder and faster, until he released himself inside of me, and I felt every ounce of it. I fell against his chest, and he lifted me up, pulling his dick out of me.

"Your juices are flowing out of me," I grinned.

"I feel you dripping and shit."

I climbed back into the passenger seat and stared at him. I asked him if I could have his jersey to put on me so it could cover the back of my dress, which I'm sure was wet from my juices. He took it off, and I marveled at his sleeve of tattoos. He handed the jersey to me, and I put it on.

"So, when are you going to come back to my house and kick it with me?" he asked after rumbling through his back seat and finding another shirt to put on.

"Um, I don't know. It's your house," I chuckled.

"We got to figure out when we going on our trip anyway. Come on, let me walk you back to your brother's car."

He got out the car and opened the door for me. He wrapped his arm around me and kept kissing me on my forehead. I couldn't help but to think that someone was watching us. Everything with him was too much like right. A businessman in school, working to own his own barber type place, his house was amazing, his ride was nice, and he had a motorcycle. He said he's not dating anyone seriously. Him opening Kade's door took my mind away from trying to find his flaws.

"Aight, take me off your block lists, aight? If not, I know where you live at," he said and smacked me on my ass.

"Aight, fam," Kade said.

"Shut up, nigga," he addressed him. "Hey, pretty girl." He leaned in the car and spoke to Kalena.

"She's fifteen, not five," I said to him.

"Shut up, hater." He kissed me on my neck and then on my lips again. "I'll talk to you later."

He shut Kade's door, and I watched him walk back to his car. Mane, his walk is so fucking sexy, Jesus Christ! Everything about him was so sexy that I just couldn't help but to think that something was off with him.

"You got it bad, sister girl," Kalena said, and pulled my earlobe.

I smiled to myself because my sister was right. I did have it bad, and I just hoped with my fingers crossed that he wasn't crazy or anything like that.

∞

"Now, I have given you time, and all you can say is that you are gaining his trust. It's been almost a month since I have given you this task, and you've been gaining his trust for that whole time," my dad said through clenched teeth.

"Dad, he is a man. How long did it take mom to gain your trust? You think that a man is just going to out the blue tell me that his dad is some kingpin or whatever you said he was. No, he's not. All he said was his dad owned a taxi cab company, and that's it. We don't even talk about his dad, and I can't bring it up or it would look fishy," I said.

"I'm seriously losing my patience with you, Kambridge," he said, slamming his closed fist on his desk. I would have jumped, but after that session with Malice in his car, I was relaxed. I guess he noticed it as well.

"You actually like the guy, don't you? You are falling for the guy. I haven't seen that white guy around here lately since I gave you that task. Did you fuck him?"

"It doesn't matter if I like him or not, or if we have had sex or not, he's still not going to divulge that type of information to me so soon."

"Soon enough to fuck, but not soon enough to get him to tell you that his dad is a drug dealer. Oh. Get out of my office before⊠"

"I'm going to invite him to dinner soon. Please be nice to him whenever he does come. You come off like the asshole you are, you will run him off, and you will never get the information that you so desperately need," I snapped.

He stood up like he was getting ready to come hit me, but I stood firm. Being around Phoenix has given me a much-needed confidence boost.

"Oh, you so smart now, huh? You so confident now to talk shit to me like I won't slap you across your face."

"If Malice sees a bruise on me, I'm not sure what he will do," I said and winked at him.

My dad started seething, and I backed out of his office. I let out the breath that I was secretly holding. I had never stood up to my dad like that before, and I'm sure I will probably never do it again. I can't believe I threatened him like that. Malice hadn't even said anything else about my dad abusing me, and I hadn't even brought it up. The only thing that was in my head was how I was going to keep stalling before my dad realized that he was not going to get any information regarding Malice.

Malice

The whole time I was at school, I was thinking about Kambridge's invitation to have dinner with her family. Mane, I'm twenty-eight years old, and I have never met nobody's parents before. All I know is that her dad is an abusive asshole ass judge, and her mom…shit, I don't even know her mom's name. Since we've been talking, she doesn't really talk about them as much. She only talks about herself and us. I could barely focus in class because of that. The only thing I could think about was her dad saying something out the way, and me knocking his ass out. I was already two seconds off his ass anyway. Luckily there haven't been any new bruises on her since the first time I saw her naked. When she falls asleep at my house, I look over her body carefully, just to make sure she ain't hiding anything from me.

After class, I headed over to my parents' house. I was supposed to come by here a week ago, but I ain't had time. Well, I could have made time, but I already know what the fuck he wanted. I pulled in the yard, and there were a few black trucks in the yard, which meant my dad was having a meeting. As soon as I walked in the house, my dad called me on the intercom to his office. Walking in his office, there were black suits crowding the office, along with Mayhem sitting in the corner on the computer. We locked eyes, but his expression was unreadable.

"Yeah, Dad!"

"Um, where are you with my shit with that lil' bitch?" he asked, not even looking at me.

My body started getting hot, and I just wanted to leap across his desk on his ass. My heart was beating so fast because I was pissed that he referred to her as a bitch, and she was not even close. I had to keep my teeth together to prevent myself from going off on him.

"Look at your lil' jawline flexing. You must have fucked her, and now you call yourself in love," he laughed.

"I don't need this. This is for you, not for me," I snapped, and turned to walk away.

"Son, I was joking, but it seems like you really have caught *feelings*. That ain't what you was supposed to do. Get the information and dump her ass."

"She doesn't talk about him, and Kam is a smart girl. She will catch on," I sighed.

"*Kam is a smart girl, she will catch on*," he mimicked me. "I don't give a damn if she was a rocket scientist. If you feeling her, then she is probably feeling you more. Get the information, and get it fast. That stupid daddy of hers locked up Frank today. Threw the book at him and gave him life with no parole. That is the fifth person this month that works for me, that he has locked up. Key people in my organization. Get the information so I can blow his fucking house up, with him inside of it."

I felt like all the air had been sucked out of me. I didn't want her to be killed. I ain't give two shits about her dad because he was a piece of shit, but I ain't want shit to happen to my Kambridge.

"You're going to kill Kambridge?" I asked just above a whisper.

"That's not my problem. Neither is it yours, once you get what I need," he said, shooing me away like I was worrisome fly.

I turned on my heels and left the office quickly because I needed some air. As soon as I stepped outside, I sat on the steps and put my hands in my palms. If I don't do this, then I would be labeled a traitor. If I do this, then I lose Kam forever. That's a fucked-up choice to have.

"Bro, you aight? This needs to happen. That man is trying to dismantle our operation, one person at a time. It's no other judge but him that's locking up our people. That cannot happen. Once you give dad what he needs, just keep Kam away from the house," Mayhem said taking a seat next to me.

"You in on this too?" I looked at him.

"I wasn't until he locked up Frank for life. He had no prior charges. Frank is my dude, and he can't sit behind bars for that shit, bro."

"Pryor, Kam loves her family, and even her dad for some odd reason. Kade and Kalena are like her best friends, and for her to lose them both at the same time, it will kill her. And then knowing that I played a part in that, would kill me too. I can't do that to her, bro. Dad must give me a sure-fire way to only kill her father, and I will get what he needs. Until then, I won't be doing anything," I said, standing up and walking away from him.

On the way to my house to get ready for this dinner date, Kam called me, and I inadvertently smiled. She really was a breath of fresh air.

"What's up, Kammy?" I answered the phone.

"Look, I am twenty-two, not two. What are you doing?"

"On my way home to get ready for the dinner. What are you doing?"

"You just crossed my mind for some odd reason. It sounds like something is wrong with you. If you don't want to come over then you don't have to. I can just tell my mom that you had something to do."

"Nah, I'm good," I lied. "I'm glad I crossed your mind. I hope all good thoughts."

"Yes, very good and nasty thoughts."

"Watch out now! I'll take you down right in the judge's house," I chuckled.

"Don't tempt me, Phoenix. I can't wait until you get here. I'm sure you are not as nervous as I am. I pray my dad doesn't embarrass me or you. Anyway, I'll let you get in the house and get dressed. Press five on the keypad, and it'll ring to my phone to let you in. Bye!" she said and hung up the phone.

Pulling my car in the garage, I mentally thought of my closet to see what I would wear to this dinner. I settled on a nice Polo shirt and some khaki chinos. I took a quick shower and put on my Issey Miyake cologne. Kam said she loved that on me. I got dressed, gave myself a once over, and left the house.

On the way over to Kam's house, I made sure to put Cat's ass on 'do not disturb' because she had been calling me like a hundred times a day for the last week. I swear I only answer about two times out of the hundred, and she don't want shit but for me to come over and fuck her. I ain't fucking her again until I know for sure that she is sane in the head, and got that relationship shit out of her head. Pulling up to Kam's gate, I pressed five, said my name, and the gate opened like two seconds later.

I pulled up behind Kam's car and got out. My heart started beating fast because I was nervous. I should have hit the blunt before I left the house. I brought it with me in case I had to take a break from her parents. I'm sure I'll probably need it after this damn dinner. I took a deep breath before I rang the doorbell. The door opened and my mouth hit the ground.

"Tracey..."

"Malice..."

"Mom..." Kambridge said from behind her.

TO BE CONTINUED

Looking for a publishing home?

Royalty Publishing House, Where the Royals reside, is accepting submissions for writers in the urban fiction genre. If you're interested, submit the first 3-4 chapters with your synopsis to submissions@royaltypublishinghouse.com.

Check out our website for more information: www.royaltypublishinghouse.com.

Text ROYALTY to 42828 to join our mailing list!

To submit a manuscript for our review, email us at
submissions@royaltypublishinghouse.com

Text RPHCHRISTIAN to 22828 for our
CHRISTIAN ROMANCE novels!

Text RPHROMANCE to 22828 for our
INTERRACIAL ROMANCE novels!

Do You Like CELEBRITY GOSSIP?

Check Out QUEEN DYNASTY!
Visit Our Site: www.thequeendynasty.com

Get LiT!

Download the LiT eReader app today and enjoy exclusive content, free books, and more

CPSIA information can be obtained
at www.ICGtesting.com
Printed in the USA
LVHW041606190919
631611LV00012B/1103